LOVE MEANS...
COURAGE

ANDREW GREY

Dreamspinner Press

Published by
Dreamspinner Press
4760 Preston Road
Suite 244-149
Frisco, TX 75034
http://www.dreamspinnerpress.com/

Love Means… Courage

Cover Design by Mara McKennen

ISBN: 978-1-61581-059-8

Printed in the United States of America
First Edition
October, 2009

eBook edition available
eBook ISBN: 978-1-61581-060-4

PROLOGUE

"MR. PARKER, are you ready with the lights?"

"Yes, Mr. Stevens, I'm ready when you are." *I've been ready for the last half hour.* He turned on the spotlight and pointed it front and center, waiting for the start of the dress rehearsal.

"Danny, Sandy, shall we begin?" The drama teacher insisted on calling everyone by their character names during rehearsals; he thought it helped people get into character. Personally, from where Len had been sitting on the lighting platform for multiple rehearsals, he thought it only confused the actors, but who was he to say anything?

A chorus of "Yes, Mr. Stevens" echoed from behind the curtains, and the rehearsal began. Len's job was to man one of the two spotlights. So he and his best friend Ruby were high on the platform, watching and following the lighting cues as the rehearsal progressed.

They'd been friends since the fifth grade, but Len thought that Ruby might have a crush on him, though he did his very best not to encourage her. She was his best friend, and he didn't want to mess that up with anything romantic. Besides, if he were honest with himself, she really wasn't his type—really, *really* wasn't his type, but he didn't allow himself to think about that much.

She leaned close, touching his arm. "I don't know why you volunteered to do this. I mean, it's cool that you did, but it doesn't seem like the type of thing you usually do." That was very true; it wasn't his usual thing, but the drama teacher, who also happened to be his English teacher, had promised extra credit to any of his students who helped with the school play.

He turned his head to Ruby for just a second. "I need anything I can get in English." Then he quickly turned his attention back to the stage, not wanting to miss any of his cues. "Besides," he whispered really softly as he positioned the spot on Sandy, "It's turning out to be fun."

It really was, but he most certainly couldn't tell Ruby exactly why. He widened the beam of light to encompass both Sandy and Danny and had to stop himself from sighing. *Jesus, you're turning into a girl.* He shook the thought out of his head before he could run with it and forced his attention back to what was happening on the stage.

Cliff Laughton was playing Danny Zuko, and all through rehearsals, Len had been thinking of him a lot. Particularly late at night when he was alone in his bed. Cliff Laughton had fueled so many fantasies over the past few weeks—mostly about what he looked like under the black leather jacket, the white T-shirt, and beneath those jeans that definitely looked a size too small.

Len pulled himself back out of his fantasy just in time to make the changes for the "Summer Lovin'" number. He quickly changed out the filters and widened the beam to include the entire stage, and the number began.

Len was enthralled. The dance movements were really seductive, particularly for the small town of Scottville, Michigan, but Len didn't know that. All he knew was that Cliff was moving his hips and shaking that tight little behind.

"She's wonderful, isn't she?"

Shit! Ruby had noticed how enthralled he'd become. He nodded his head and breathed a sigh of relief. She thought he was entranced with Sheila Gowell, the girl playing Sandy, and that was fine with Len. "Yes, she is."

Personally, he thought Sheila was a scene-stealing, over-acting cow, but he wasn't about to tell Ruby that. He couldn't afford for anyone to get the wrong idea. He knew he had to keep these feelings to himself. This may be 1979, but it wasn't New York or San Francisco—it was Scottville, Michigan, and the very idea of anyone knowing he might be interested in boys was enough to send chills down his spine.

"It's going very well, don't you think?" Ruby had scooted closer, leaning against the railing as the action continued on the stage.

He kept his voice extremely low so it wouldn't travel. "Yes, it is." He smiled at her from over the spotlight and concentrated on the play and his cues.

At intermission, he climbed down from the lighting platform and walked to where the drama teacher was standing near the stage. "Do you want any changes?"

"No, everything looked great." Len felt the man's hand on his shoulder. "Keep up the good work." Len was about to turn around and head back to the platform, when he saw Cliff at the edge of the stage.

"Mr. Stevens," Cliff called as he jumped off the stage and lost his balance, barreling into Len and knocking him flat on his back with Cliff landing on top of him. Len could barely breathe, and not just because Cliff had knocked the wind out of him. He could feel Cliff's warmth through his clothes, and when he opened his eyes, he was looking right into Cliff's. And to his surprise, Cliff was looking back and didn't turn away. His eyes were soft and warm; his breath smelled like Tic Tac. Len felt himself react and began to squirm. It would be the ultimate in embarrassment—hell, he'd never live it down if Cliff felt him get a stiffie.

"Cliff... Len... are you two all right?" The activity around them broke the last of the spell that had held them.

Cliff lifted himself off Len and got to his feet. "I'm fine, but I landed on Len here." He turned his attention to Len, who was still sprawled on the floor. "You okay?" He extended his hand, and Len took it, slowly getting to his feet.

"I'm okay, just a little winded." *And immensely relieved that you aren't reacting and apparently didn't feel anything.* "I'll be fine." The emphasis shifted from him to the second act of the play, and Len listened to the instructions before walking to the back of the gym and climbing the lighting platform.

Ruby stood and met him as took his place by the light. "Are you okay?"

"Yeah, I'm fine."

"Okay, boys and girls, let's run through the second act!" The ceiling lights dimmed, and Len turned on the spotlight, trying concentrate on the stage. His mind, however, was definitely elsewhere. Cliff Laughton. He'd actually felt Cliff Laughton's body on top of his. Granted, Cliff had fallen, but that didn't really seem to matter one bit to his active imagination and hormone-crazed body. It reacted with gusto, but luckily it was dark, and no one could see him except Ruby, whose attention was glued to the stage. He let his mind wander for a minute but then stopped himself as the guilt kicked in. *I shouldn't be having thoughts like this. I can't. I just can't.*

Love Means ... *Courage*

Ruby turned her attention from the stage. "What did you say?" Len shook his head, and she turned back to the rehearsal.

As the show progressed, Len remembered all his cues, taking a break as the scene was being changed to the drive-in. The lights were low with just his light shining on Danny and Sandy as he tried to make out with her in the car. Len's mind took him on a flight of fantasy as he imagined himself in the car with Cliff, those hands all over him. As he watched the scene, he knew that he wouldn't push him away, not if he thought he could get away with it.

He almost missed his next cue and had to quickly change the filters and adjust the light, but he made it just in time. That near miss kept his mind sharp for the rest of the rehearsal, and everything went smoothly.

At the end of the rehearsal, Len turned off the light, and let it cool before helping Ruby off the platform. Everyone was gathered around the stage, talking animatedly, the excitement in their voices plain to hear.

"Len." He turned and saw Cliff striding his way. Len stopped and waited for him to approach. "Just wanted to make sure I didn't hurt you."

Len shook his head. "No, I'm fine."

Cliff smiled a bright, open smile and said, "After the last performance on Saturday we're having a wrap party at my house. You should be there."

"Thanks." Cliff just stood there, and Len wondered if he had more he wanted to say. The silence started to grow uncomfortable. "I'll plan on it," Len added.

"Good." Cliff hesitated again. "Good." Cliff shoved his hands into his pockets. "I was—"

Whatever Cliff was about to say was cut off as Sheila swished in and grabbed Cliff's arm. "There you are. I'm ready to go, and you were going to give me a ride home." She basically ignored Len and pulled Cliff to where some of her friends were waiting. Len saw Cliff turn his head briefly back toward him, and then he was gone.

"You know Cliff Laughton?" Ruby asked as she came up behind him. "Too bad that bitch Sheila's got her claws in him." Len turned around, surprised at the language. "Well, she is," Ruby continued, "and he's too nice to tell her to get lost. Maybe you could introduce us." Len knew that Ruby had had a crush on Cliff Laughton since the seventh grade.

"He just asked me if I was okay and invited me to the wrap party on Saturday." He turned to her, letting his attention fall from where Cliff had disappeared. "Would you like to go with me?"

She smiled her biggest, brightest smile and took Len's arm. "I'd love to." She actually batted her eyes at him until they both laughed, and together they headed outside and waited for his mother to pick them up.

LEN'S mother dropped him and Ruby at the party on Saturday, but not after grilling them like a CIA agent would. "If there's alcohol, you both stay away and call me. I'll come right back and pick you up." Len's mother could be formidable, and neither of them had any thoughts about crossing her. "I'll pick you both up at eleven."

"Okay, Mom." Len helped Ruby out of the car, "We'll be fine." He deliberately kept himself from rolling his eyes; she'd pick up on that. The woman picked up on everything.

The party was obviously in the yard. A fire had been lit, and there were tables with food and drinks nearby. Most of the cast was already there, and they walked up and said hello. He knew everybody. Mason County Central High School wasn't big enough for you to not know everyone.

"Hey, Len. Hi, Ruby." Cliff greeted them both and showed them where everything was with Sheila sticking to him like glue.

The school musical had been a huge success, with every performance nearly sold out, and during those weeks of rehearsal, the cast members had become quite close. "Are you two going to prom?" Len turned around and saw Brenda, one of the Pink Ladies, asking as she approached.

"No, I have to work." Len knew that Ruby was disappointed, but he hadn't wanted her to miss it. "But Ruby's going with Brad." Brenda giggled and pulled Ruby away, leading her over to where the girls were talking. It never ceased to amaze Len that they all went to school together every day, sat in the same classrooms, and ate lunch together, but put them in a social setting, and the girls and boys separated like milk and cream.

Len wandered over to where the guys were talking, hearing Cliff's voice over the rest. "She's driving me crazy, thinks I'm her boyfriend or something. Is she delusional? I'm not Danny, and she's not Sandy. The play's over."

"So break it off with her. Tell her you're not interested, because she sure thinks you are." Cliff was about to say something when one of the other guys chimed in. "I heard she puts out."

Cliff snorted and laughed. "Are you kidding? She's some sort of nun." Then Cliff made a face that Len couldn't see, and everyone laughed. The girls made their way over, and the party shifted as couples paired off. Ruby was talking to Brad, and Len was pleased the two of them were getting along. Ruby was a friend, and he knew she would never be more than that. The mere thought of anything more than that scared him.

Len stayed near the food table, talking with the guys. He was having a great time. The night was cool but not cold, and everyone was friendly and sociable. Throughout the evening, he watched as the occasional couple snuck off onto one of the paths for a little private partying.

"Len." He turned and saw Cliff coming over sans Sheila. "Do you have a minute?"

"Sure."

Cliff motioned behind one of the barns, and Len followed, wondering what Cliff could want. "I wanted to ask you something." Cliff shifted from foot to foot, his nervousness apparent. "The other day—" He stopped and then started over. "During dress rehearsal, when I knocked you over...."

Len was ready for the earth to swallow him whole. *Cliff had felt him.* How in the world was he going to explain it away? "Listen, Cliff, it was an accident...." He began to stammer and look around, trying to determine the best way to disappear.

"I know. I didn't mean to knock you over. I felt bad that I might have hurt you. Mr. Stevens reamed me a good one the next day."

Len slowly released the breath he'd been holding. "No, I just got the wind knocked out of me, but that didn't last long." He heard his normal tone return to his voice.

Cliff leaned close, his face near Len's. "I'm glad. I thought I might have damaged something important, if you know what I mean."

Len's first and only instinct was to play dumb. "Huh?"

"I felt you." Cliff's eyes rose to meet his, and Len was surprised at what he didn't see. There was no disgust, no condemnation, and no world coming to an end. Len swallowed and

Love Means ... *Courage*

waited to see what Cliff would do. He braced himself for the worst. Instead, he saw Cliff looking at him, their eyes locked onto each others'. Len thought he saw Cliff getting closer and wondered if he was going to kiss him. Len's lips parted, and he saw Cliff tilt his head just slightly. He closed his eyes and felt a light touch on his lips. *Damn, he was kissing Cliff Laughton, or Cliff was kissing him. It didn't really matter; this was like a dream come true.*

"Cliff!" Sheila's voice cut through the night like a knife. They pulled away and straightened up just as she rounded the corner of the barn. "I've been looking for you everywhere." At that point she noticed Len. "Hey, Len."

God damn it! Why'd she have to show up now? Len wanted to scream. He composed himself quickly, wiping the disappointment from his face. "Hi, Sheila."

She latched onto Cliff's arm and began walking him away, obviously unaware of what had almost happened, and what she'd almost seen.

Cliff tried to take control of the conversation. "Sheila, we need to talk."

"I'll say we do. There are some things we definitely need to get settled for after graduation." The girl was driven; you had to give her credit for that. She knew what she wanted and went for it, no holds barred.

Len watched as they walked away, and he again saw Cliff turn to look at him. And this time, there was nothing in the way. What he saw surprised him, because it looked like disappointment.

Len got a hold of himself again and walked from behind the barn to rejoin the party. Ruby and Brad were still sitting together talking. He checked his watch; their ride wouldn't be there for another half hour, so he sat quietly around the fire, making small talk with other people he knew. One of the girls whispered in his ear, "Are you okay with Ruby and Brad?"

Len turned and smiled. "Ruby and I are good friends." He heard a car pull into the driveway and realized it was his ride. He'd been hoping to see Cliff again before he left, but he was nowhere to be seen, although Sheila had returned to the party, definitely looking subdued. Len said his good-byes and got Ruby, and the two of them climbed in the car.

His mother asked all about the party, and Ruby told her everything that happened. As they pulled out of the drive, Len craned his head, trying to see Cliff, until the farm disappeared into the night.

CHAPTER 1

LEN woke slowly from his doze, Tim's arms holding him, their shared warmth taking away the slight chill from the air conditioning. He liked it here, right where he was, right now. No pressure, no expectations, no hiding, just a few hours of what felt like stolen happiness. He started to get out of bed, but Tim's arms tightened around him slightly. "Why the rush, Lenny?"

He didn't know what to say, other than it just felt like the right thing to do. "I don't know." It was their usual behavior.

Tim shifted on his bed, looking down at him. "I do." Len was surprised but wasn't sure how to react. "You don't want me to get the wrong idea," Tim said.

"And what idea is that?" Len looked at the older man's face, taking in the slight crinkles around the eyes and the hairline that was just starting to recede. It was a handsome, warm, gentle face that matched the rest of him.

"You don't want me to think this is anything more than it is. We get together every few weeks, watch a movie, have dinner, and then fall into bed together. You like that; I like that. But when it's over, you feel like you need to leave." Tim looked so disappointed that Len leaned forward to kiss that look away, but Tim didn't let him. "I know I'm not the love of your life—you're twenty-one, and I'm nearly forty. You've got your whole life ahead of you." He stopped, and Len waited for him to continue. Tim sighed. "I don't know what I'm trying to say, other than the fact that you don't need to rush off. I'm not going to fall in love with you in the next half hour."

"I just didn't want to be unfair to you. You've been a good friend," Len tried to explain. Tim had been a *great* friend. Len had met him a year earlier while he was cruising the gay magazine section of the only newsstand in the entire county that carried things like that. He'd been horny beyond belief, and he'd watched as a handsome older man entered the store and walked to the same section where Len was leafing through magazines, trying to keep his embarrassment under control. Tim had told him later that he'd looked into Len's scared face and almost laughed. But instead of laughing, Tim had talked to him, really talked to him. It was one of the first times in his life that Len had realized that there were other men like him. Men who liked other men but didn't dress like women, act all froofy, or lisp. They acted normally.

After talking to him for a while, Tim had asked, "Would you like to get a cup of coffee?" Len must have looked like a deer in headlights because Tim continued with, "It's only coffee, and we can talk."

"Okay." Len was nervous, but he'd followed the man out of the store and down the street to a small café where they got a table in the corner. Tim had introduced himself, and they'd talked. Well, Tim talked, and Len listened. When they'd finished their coffee, Tim had given Len his phone number and told him to call if he wanted to talk again. Len had just held the card as he watched Tim leave the café.

Love Means ... *Courage*

He'd called him a few days later, they'd gotten together for dinner, and things had progressed from there.

Len shifted on the bed, slinking his arms around Tim's neck. "You're one of the best people I've ever met."

Tim grinned. "No, I'm not. I'm an old man who gets to sample some of your energy every once in a while." Len knew from Tim's smile that there was some grain of truth in what he'd said.

Len lightly swatted Tim's side. "Yes you are." He really was a good person. Tim had shown him a lot, not just in the bedroom, and had helped him accept who he was. "You've been a good friend."

"So have you." Len felt Tim kiss him on the forehead, and then the bed dipped as Tim got up. Len followed suit and began to get dressed. Something was different, and as Len pulled on his pants, he realized that Tim was sending him on his way. Len thought over how he felt about it as he finished dressing.

"I'm going to miss you." Len sat on the edge of the bed and tied his shoes.

"I'm going to miss you, too, but it's probably best for both of us," Tim said. Len finished dressing and stood near the foot of the bed, looking at Tim dressed in his robe. Tim pulled him into a deep hug, holding him tight, and Len got the feeling this was harder for Tim than he was letting on. After a long while, he felt Tim's arms relax. "I'll walk you to the door." Tim led him out of the bedroom and through the small apartment. It was then that he noticed the boxes stacked on the corners.

"Are you moving?" That explained some things.

"Yeah. I got a good job in Chicago, and I can't turn it down, not in this economy."

"I understand." Len opened the door. "Bye, Tim."

"Bye, Lenny. Be happy." Len turned and smiled as the apartment door closed with a soft click. He would be. More than anything else, Tim had helped him admit to himself, without really realizing it, that he was gay. He wasn't ready to share that knowledge with other people yet, but at least he could admit it to himself, and he no longer hated himself because of it. Tim had told him once that there was nothing wrong with being gay or being who you were. He'd just warned him that he needed to be careful.

Without looking back, Len walked to his car, climbed into the driver's seat, and headed home. He did a quick check of his Timex and breathed a sigh of relief. It wasn't too late, and he probably wouldn't get the third degree from his mother.

After graduating from high school, he'd gotten a job at a small factory making parts for railroad cars, but that had only lasted a year before he'd been laid off because of the tanking economy. His mother had urged him to go back to school, and he'd followed her advice, attending the local community college. It had been a good decision. Len had been a mediocre student in high school, but he seemed to thrive in the college environment. His grades were good, and he was working part-time after classes mucking out stalls at one of the area horse farms.

Pulling into their driveway, he parked the car next to the small house they rented and headed inside. His mother was sitting in the small living room watching television. "Did you have a good time?"

Len had to stop himself from smiling too big. "Yes, thanks." He'd had some time to think on the way home, and while he would definitely miss Tim, he was happy that he'd found a good job. And Tim had been right: it was time for both of them to move on before either got too attached. Tim had been a wonderful mentor, and Len would never forget him.

"There's some mail on the table for you. Looks like you got a wedding invitation."

Love Means ... *Courage*

"From who?" She shrugged her shoulders and went back to the television. She worked hard, always had, and he wished he could help out more. But every time he talked about trying to get a full-time job, she'd scold him and tell him to finish school first.

Len went into the kitchen and saw the large, fancy envelope sitting on the table. He picked it up, looking it over before breaking the seal, opening the envelope, and removing the invitation. "Ruby's getting married," he called to his mother.

"That's great; who's the lucky boy?" Her attention didn't waver from the television.

"Cliff Laughton." Well, damn him if that wasn't a surprise. He hadn't seen Cliff much since he was seventeen, but his mind wandered back to the night of the school musical cast party and the almost-kiss—or what he thought might have been an almost-kiss. With the passage of time, he wasn't so sure.

"When is it?"

He consulted the invitation. "Three weeks."

"Are you going to go?"

He thought about it. He hadn't seen Ruby in a while, but yeah, it would be real nice to see her again. "I think so."

THE wedding was beautiful, held in the country church a mile or so from Cliff's family's farm and what was to be Ruby's new home. There were a lot of people there who Len knew. When he'd accepted the invitation, he'd wondered if he'd still know anyone. But for the most part, it seemed as though time hadn't moved, and everyone was very interested in catching up with old friends. After the service, he drove to the reception and found his place at one of the tables, along with a number of people he'd been friends with years before. It was almost like a mini-reunion.

He felt a gentle nudge in his side. "So, Len, are you seeing anyone?" Raelyn beamed at him from the next seat.

"Not right now." He thought of Tim. "I was for a while."

"You remember Brenda Grant?" Len nodded and tried to look interested. He'd had so many people try to fix him up lately, and it was starting to become tiresome. "She just broke up with Brad and was talking about looking you up." Thank God she hadn't called.

He made what he thought was a bland, noncommittal reply. "It'd be nice to hear from her again."

Raelyn beamed. "I'll have to tell her." Len almost groaned but kept it to himself, and the conversation shifted to other topics and local gossip before being cut off by the tinkling of glasses to indicate that it was time for the speeches. The best man gave his speech and offered the toast, and then dinner was served, followed by the usual wedding games.

Len watched as Cliff danced his new bride around the floor, both of them smiling and happy. Seeing them together, Len let his mind wander back, and he thought that he'd been a fool. Tim had told him once never to fall for a straight man. And while Len was never sure what would have happened if they hadn't been interrupted that evening, more and more, he was coming to realize that it must have been his imagination. Then the first dance ended, and the floor filled with couples.

After a while, the bride's dance was announced, and Len got in line and paid his money. He saw Ruby smile as he approached and started to dance with her. "I was so happy you decided to come."

"Me too. I've been looking forward to seeing you since I got the invitation." They moved together easily; they always had.

Love Means ... *Courage*

"Are you seeing anyone?"

"I was, but I'm not now." It was an easy answer that rolled off his tongue. He knew he was playing up the casual thing he'd had with Tim, but he needed something to hide behind.

"What was he like?" Len heard her clearly and almost stumbled, but Ruby just smiled and kept dancing, tightening her grip on his hand.

"How...?" He forced his body to keep moving, even as he felt his stomach tighten and the chicken from dinner try to make a reappearance.

"How did I know? It wasn't one thing." She grinned. "But I've known for a while." Her smile remained. "It's okay. I'd never tell anyone."

"Does Cliff know?"

Her smile brightened. "Good God, no. Are you kidding? He's got a bigger mouth than Sheila." Her smile faded a little. "I think it's cool, and I'd never tell anyone, but I wanted to let you know that it doesn't matter, that you're still my friend, and that I've missed you."

Before he could say anything more, he felt a tap on his shoulder indicating that his time was up. He let go of her hand and was about to step away, but instead he leaned forward and gently kissed her cheek, "You're quite a lady." Then he stepped away and let the next man in line dance with the bride.

On his way back to his chair, he made a point to say hello to Cliff. To Len's surprise, he remembered him.

"Len, I'm glad you could come."

"Thanks. I'm glad you invited me." He glanced at the bride, who was now dancing with a very old man. "She's really something. I sincerely hope you'll be happy."

17

"Thanks."

Len wasn't sure what else to say. He most certainly wasn't about to mention the short kiss they'd shared—that he thought they'd shared—those years ago. So he shook the groom's hand and headed back to his table. After a while, the lights dimmed again, and the dancing continued. The bride and groom made their way around to the tables, talking with everyone and accepting good wishes. After a brief stop at the table the happy couple moved on, and Len decided to call it a night. He said good night to everyone and then headed to his car and drove home.

His mother was sitting in the living room, watching the end of a *Fantasy Island* rerun. She turned and smiled as he came inside. "Was the wedding nice?"

"Yes, very nice. The food was good, and I danced with the bride. We didn't really get a chance to catch up, but she said she'd call in the next few weeks so we could get together." He sat on the sofa, loosening his tie, half watching the end of the program and half watching her.

The show came to an end, and she got up and turned off the television, "I'm going to miss that show when they take it off the air in a few months." It was his mother's favorite show; she never missed it. "Is there something on your mind?"

"Well, kind of...." Ruby's candid revelation about him had thrown him for a loop. He'd always been close to his mom, and it didn't feel right to keep secrets from her, particularly when someone else knew. He was just worried how she'd react.

She sat next to him and patted his knee. "It's okay, honey, just tell me what's wrong."

He wasn't sure of the right way to say it, so in the end, he just blurted it out. "Mom, I'm gay." He turned to look at her reaction, and she sat there unmoving for a split second.

Love Means ... *Courage*

"Is that all? I thought you were going to tell me something I didn't already know."

Len was taken aback. "You knew. Geez, does everybody know?"

"I don't think so, and what do you mean everybody?"

"Ruby told me when I was dancing with her." This was not the reaction he was expecting from her, but he was thankful for it nonetheless. If he were honest with himself, he wasn't sure what he'd expected.

"I can't speak for Ruby, but I can tell you that a mother knows her children." She yawned and got up. "I'm going to bed." She bent down and kissed him on the forehead before leaving the room. "I'll see you in the morning, and we'll talk."

Len sat on the sofa, thinking. He'd had his deepest, darkest secret opened to two people, and they hadn't rejected him. He knew it wouldn't always be so easy, but it gave him hope. Getting up, he turned off the light and went to bed.

CHAPTER 2

ALMOST to Len's surprise, Ruby did call him a few weeks later. Len was just finishing up spring semester classes, so they agreed to meet in the college cafeteria for lunch. After getting their food, they sat at one of the corner tables overlooking the ravine and creek behind the building.

"So, I'm dying to know, are you seeing anyone?" She took a bite of her salad, eyes wide with excitement.

"No. I was seeing someone casually, but he left town." Len began eating, watching for her reaction.

"I'm sorry."

He could see the empathy in her eyes. "It wasn't like that. I'm going to miss his friendship more than anything." He took another bite and swallowed. "He's the first person I met who understood how I feel." She nodded and remained quiet. "I told my mother when I got home from the wedding," he added.

Ruby's smile faded. "How'd she take it?"

Love Means ... *Courage*

"Really well. She said she already knew, kissed me, and then went to bed. We had a good talk the next afternoon. I don't think she fully understands, but she's being supportive, and that's all I can ask for." He took a drink of his soda. "Enough about me, tell me about you. How's married life? How did you and Cliff meet?"

She smiled a huge, happy smile that warmed Len's heart. Ruby had always been someone special, and he'd regretted not staying in touch after graduation. It was his fault; he'd never kept in touch with anyone. He'd become so insular. The need to protect his secret seemed to overtake everything else, leaving him afraid to get close to anyone. "After graduation, I met Cliff again at my sister's wedding reception. He's a friend of my brother-in-law. Neither of us was seeing anyone at the time, and I'd always thought he was handsome. After spending most of the evening talking, he asked me out, and as they say, the rest is history. He's really wonderful."

Len watched as her face lit with happiness. "Where are you living?"

"For now, we're staying with his parents. The farmhouse is so huge, but we're saving for our own house." She pulled a face. "His father's okay but so controlling. No wonder his mother left years ago. I don't think I could take being married to that man either. He's so old fashioned." Ruby smiled wickedly. "He actually expects me to do all the cooking because I'm a woman." She leaned forward. "When we got home from our honeymoon, we went to dinner at my parents', and he actually asked me what I was cooking for him." She started laughing. "I told him I hadn't married him, and that Steve's Bar was open until midnight, and then I threw his keys at him. He was still sputtering when we left the house."

Len couldn't help joining in her laughter; it was so infectious. He'd missed this—missed her energy and her sense of humor. She was still the same person he remembered, but now more confident and sure of herself, without all the teenage angst and worry. He also found it surprisingly comfortable to have someone he could be himself with, someone he didn't need to hide from.

Their laughter subsided, and she leaned forward, looking around to make sure no one was nearby. "So tell me about this guy you were seeing. Was he nice?"

"Yes, he was. His name was Tim, and he was…" he hesitated. "Older than me."

That wicked smirk was back. "How much older?"

"He was almost forty."

Her reaction was not at all what Len was expecting. "Was he hot?"

Now it was Len's turn to laugh. "Are you getting a thrill out of this?"

"Of course. Two men together is sexy. Now spill it."

He could not believe he was sitting in the college cafeteria with one of his high school friends talking about his love life. "He was hot, if you must know, but he was also kind. More than anything, he showed me that I wasn't alone, that there were other people like me. But above all, he was a friend."

"Did you love him?"

"I guess, but I wasn't *in love* with him, if that makes any sense. We both knew that what we had was temporary, and we parted as friends. It's not like it was some big traumatic breakup or anything." It had been hard for Len, but not in a way he expected. He still missed the friendship and closeness he'd had with Tim, along with the fact that he could relax with the older man and just be himself. Well, that along with the amazing sex, but he wasn't about to tell Ruby that. Hell, the girl would probably want details, and there was no way he was providing those.

Love Means ... *Courage*

Len checked his watch and was surprised how fast the time had flown. "I have to be in class in fifteen minutes." She stood up, and he took their trash, throwing it away before returning the trays. "I'll walk you to the car." He picked up his books and jacket before leading the way through the building and out to the parking lot. "It was great to see you." He wasn't sure what to do, but she took care of that when she hugged him.

"It was fun. I'll call you soon, and we can have dinner." She smirked as she got in the car, "I promise I won't cook." They both laughed as she closed the car door and pulled out of the parking lot. He watched as she left and then turned and walked to his next class.

R<small>UBY</small> did call, and they got together every few weeks, sometimes for lunch and sometimes for dinner with both her and Cliff. It was nice to get out and have someone to talk with. And while dinners with the three of them were fun, he much preferred having lunch with just Ruby where the two of them could talk.

About a year after the wedding, she met him for lunch, bounding into the cafeteria with a special spring in her step. Len noticed and smiled, wondering what was up. "Sit down and tell me what's got you so happy you could burst."

She sat but seemed to barely touch the chair. "I'm pregnant." Her smile was radiant. "I'm due in July. I hope it's a girl, but Cliff is hoping for a boy, of course."

"Of course." He got up and gave her a hug. She seemed almost electric with energy; she was so happy. "What would you like?"

"Something light. The morning sickness has been awful, but my doctor tells me that should pass soon." She looked toward the menu board. "What I'd really like is a big juicy hamburger; morning sickness be damned. But I'll have a salad."

"That kid can't live on lettuce. You're eating for two, so get the burger." She bounced in the chair and agreed. Len got the food, returning a few minutes later.

"If it's a girl, I'm going to name her Bethany, but I haven't thought of boys' names yet. I'm thinking that if it's a boy, I'll let Cliff choose a name." She took a bite of the burger and moaned softly as she chewed.

"What does he think about being a father?" Len began eating his own lunch.

"To tell you the truth, I wasn't sure how he was going to react, but he was amazingly happy when I told him." She giggled. "Then he pulled me upstairs." She smirked and took another bite of her hamburger.

"So, it's okay for me to tell you about my love life, as pitiful as it is, but you're going to clam up about yours?" Not that he was really interested in the details, but he had to give her a little grief.

"Speaking of your love life, have you met anyone?" She asked the same question every time they got together. He swore she was going to start trolling bars around town trying to find him a nice boy.

"No, but I haven't really been looking. I've got school, and I'm working whenever I can. Hopefully, when I'm done here, I can get a decent job somewhere, but it's not looking very good. I may need to move somewhere else in order to make a decent living." He decided he really wanted to change the subject. "So how are things with Cliff's dad? He still giving you a hard time?"

She grinned. "Nope. He doesn't ask me to cook anymore, and I don't feed him food that tastes like crap."

Love Means ... *Courage*

"Can you cook anything?"

"I can make cereal."

"Like oatmeal?"

"Cornflakes." They both laughed. He always laughed when she was around. It brightened his day whenever they got together. He continued eating as he watched her wolf down the burger. Good God, that woman could eat. In all the years he'd known her, he'd rarely seen her eat anything other than a salad. Pregnancy must agree with her.

"Are you having a baby shower?"

"My friend Barbara is probably planning one, but I think she wants it to be a surprise." Len made a note to himself to try to find something special for both her and the baby. They continued talking until it was time for him to go back to class. As usual, he walked her to her car.

"How much longer do you have until you graduate?"

"One more semester. I should be done in December."

She opened her car door and climbed inside. "We'll have to have a party to celebrate." He smiled and said nothing as she closed the door and drove away.

"HE'S adorable." Len looked into the baby carrier as Ruby set it on the chair between them. "I can't believe you were actually brave enough to let Cliff name him."

"I know, and I can't believe he picked something as normal as Geoff. Not Jeffrey, but Geoff." She fussed with the sleeping baby's blanket as she took her chair. "It could have been worse. He talked about naming him after his father and calling him Howard. All in all, he made a good choice." She returned her attention to the baby. "Didn't he, Geoffy?" He was still asleep but gripped her finger and tried to suck on it.

"He looks like you." He really did. Sweet and cute with huge eyes and a head of light blond curls.

She smiled, and he got up to get their lunch, but she stopped him. "I'll get it, if you'll stay with him." Len nodded and turned his attention to the stirring baby.

"Hello, little guy." Geoff's eyes opened slowly, and he stirred a little, his hands clenching into fists that went right toward his mouth, little booted feet stretching and kicking slightly. Len held out a finger, and the baby gripped it loosely and started to squirm. He didn't cry, which was very good, and stared up at Len, eyes wide with curiosity. "You hungry? You are, aren't you?" Len turned and saw Ruby making her way back. "Lunch is on the way." She set down the trays and took her seat. "I think he's hungry."

"It's been two hours, so he probably is." Ruby picked him out of the carrier and took a blanket out of the diaper bag. Len turned and started to eat while Ruby got everything situated. When he turned back, the baby was positioned against her under the blanket, obviously having his lunch. "How have you been? Seeing anyone?"

"No, but I'm almost done with school. Just another few days of classes and then finals." He turned his attention to his food, trying not to stare.

"Do you have a job yet?"

"I wish, but I have a few interviews later this week, and I'm hopeful I'll get something. Mom has been working so hard, and she deserves a break."

Love Means … *Courage*

"Have you thought about moving out?" She shifted the baby beneath the blanket.

"Yeah, but she needs me right now. And once I'm working, I'll be able to help with some of the bills. Give her a chance to get ahead, you know." Len continued eating and Ruby picked at her salad while she fed the baby. After a while, she shifted him under the blanket, and after some futzing, which Len didn't want to know about, she set him back in the carrier, and the baby promptly fell asleep. "Does he sleep through the night?"

"Not yet, but he's getting close." She started to eat in earnest now that the baby was settled. "So why aren't you seeing anyone?" She looked around. "This is a college; there have to be other gay men." She lowered her voice so they wouldn't be overheard.

"I know, but I'm just not really interested in dating right now." The truth was he was afraid of being rejected; he wasn't sure how to approach anyone. And how did he know if anyone else might be interested anyway? He felt so awkward and unsure of himself.

"You can't keep yourself—" She was interrupted when someone approached their table.

"Ruby? That is you."

"Hi, Janelle. Do you know Len Parker? He and I went to high school together."

"I don't believe so. It's nice to meet you. I'm Cliff's sister." They exchanged pleasantries, and Len invited Janelle to sit down. They talked together until the baby began to fuss, and Ruby excused herself, telling them that she needed to get him home.

Len stood, hugged her good-bye, and handed her a wrapped box from his bag. She smiled and tore off the wrapping. Inside were a small blue sweater and some smooth wooden alphabet blocks. "My mother knitted the sweater, and I made the blocks." Ruby hugged him tightly, looking like she was going to cry. Then she turned and packed everything away.

"I'll talk to you soon," Ruby said as she turned to Janelle. They exchanged air kisses, and then she was gone, putting a blanket over the carrier before heading outside.

Len and Janelle sat together talking until it was time for his next class. "Weren't you in my public speaking class last semester?"

She smiled and nodded. "I think I was. You gave the talk on insomnia."

"And you gave a speech about the rise of computers."

They laughed and wondered aloud how they'd never met before. She'd finished her lunch, and since they were heading to the same building, they walked together.

LEN graduated and got a job working in the business office of a car dealership, handling paperwork and helping with the books. It wasn't his ideal job, but it was full-time and came with benefits. He would occasionally have lunch with Ruby, but his schedule was now more regimented. However, they did talk more often, and he heard all about how Geoff was growing.

Len had been working at the dealership for almost a year, when having lunch in the employee lounge one day, he glanced at a newspaper someone had left on the table. Flipping it open, he began to read the headlines. About a paragraph into the story, he gasped and dropped his fork. Ruby had been riding with her father-in-law, and he'd taken a curve too sharply. The car had spun out of control and hit a tree. Neither of them had survived.

CHAPTER 3

A KNOCK on his door woke him from a sound sleep. "Len, you'll be late for work."

"Shit!" He glanced at the clock and breathed a sigh of relief. He still had time. "Thanks, Ma."

"You're welcome, hon." He heard her footsteps recede as he threw back the covers and got himself out of bed, pulled on his pants, and headed to the bathroom down the hall.

"Breakfast will be ready in a few minutes," she called.

"Thanks." He cleaned up quickly and finished dressing before heading to the kitchen. Coffee was already poured, and the toast popped up just as he sat down. A few minutes later, two plates appeared on the table, and his mother sat down across from him.

"You okay, Len? You've been so quiet for so long."

A sigh escaped before he could stop it. "I still miss Ruby sometimes." He really did. She had been the one person he could talk to about anything. Oh, his mom had been supportive and tried her best to understand, but it was tough for her, and Len knew that. He also knew that she was disappointed that he wouldn't get married and that she wouldn't have grandchildren. But he missed the easy conversation he'd had with his best friend.

"I know you do, but Janelle seems nice." His mother knew he was gay, but sometimes, she just couldn't help hoping. Len didn't fault her for that. He couldn't, because there were times that he hoped as well—hoped he could be normal, like everyone else.

Len shrugged and sipped his coffee. "She's very nice, and we have fun, but she's not like Ruby." No one was like Ruby. He sometimes thought that if he was ever going to marry a woman, it would be Ruby, except for the sex part.

"I know. It's hard when you lose your best friend. Imagine how hard it's been for Cliff, losing his wife. Have you seen him since the funeral?" She began eating.

"A few times in town. I saw him last week with Geoff. He's the spitting image of his mother, and he's walking now. It was so cute seeing him walking along, holding his dad's hand." He finished his breakfast and put the dishes in the sink. "Today's payday, and I thought I'd take you to dinner."

"Don't you have plans with Janelle?"

"God, yes, I'd completely forgotten." He raced back to his bedroom and got his things for work. "I'll see you later."

He heard a muffled reply from his mother's room as he closed the door and headed out to his car. It took him about ten minutes to drive to work, WKLA providing the morning news and weather. He arrived a few minutes later than usual and parked in his regular spot, entering the dealership through the service entrance and turning on the lights in the business office before getting everything ready for the day.

Love Means ... *Courage*

The day was busy and went unusually quickly for a Friday. Just before lunch, he received a call from Janelle, confirming dinner for that evening and letting him know that she'd meet him at the restaurant at six. He'd just hung up the phone when he saw the owner of the dealership standing by the door to the office. "Len, could I speak with you a minute?"

"Sure." He had been handing out paychecks as people stopped by, so he put the remainder in the desk drawer. He looked at Keith, the business manager, and saw the look on his face. He knew that look; he'd seen it before. Taking and releasing a deep breath, he followed the boss to his front corner office.

"Please have a seat." Len sat in one of the chairs and waited. "This is something I've tried to avoid." The big man leaned forward, meeting Len's eyes. "As you know, business hasn't been very good the last few months, and while I've been hoping it would turn around, it hasn't, and I'm afraid we're going to have to let you go."

Len had heard those words before, and the second time hurt just as much as the first. Both times he'd been working for over a year, and both times he'd just started to fit in and make a few friends, have people to eat lunch with. "I understand."

"Look, Len, I'm really sorry. You've done good work, and this has nothing to do with your job performance." He passed an envelope across the desk. "When business picks up, I'd be more than happy to bring you back. You're a good worker. The envelope contains a sterling letter of recommendation and a month's severance pay along with your week of vacation pay." He stood up, and Len did the same. "I'm really sorry."

Len didn't know what to do, so he did the only thing he could think of, he held out his hand. The boss shook it, and then Len left the office, going right back to his desk, where Keith was waiting. "I'm real sorry, Len."

"Me too."

Keith checked his watch. "Get your things together and go home." He opened his desk drawer and retrieved his own paycheck from the stack of envelopes.

"Thank you for everything, Keith." He gathered his things and quietly left the building after saying a few good-byes.

The drive home was amazingly short, and no one was about as he pulled into the yard and parked the car. Walking into the house, he put his things on the table and sat in the small living room. "You'll live. It's happened before." Len got up and went into the kitchen, opening the refrigerator and taking out a beer. Pulling the pull tab, he heard the familiar pop and then the carbonation took over. Lifting the cold can to his lips, he took a big gulp as he walked back into the living room and sat down with a sigh.

The front door opened and closed, and he heard his mother come inside. "You're going to be late for your dinner if you don't get a move on."

Len stood up and met her in the kitchen. "I got laid off today." He showed her the letter and told her what they'd said.

"I'm sorry, hon. Maybe you should call Janelle and cancel."

Something inside Len bucked him up. "No. I can't let this get me down. I made plans, and I'm going to stick to them. And on Monday, I'll start looking for another job. I've been through this before, and hell, I'll probably go through it again." Just saying the words helped him feel better, so he put the last of the beer in the sink and went to his room to change clothes.

A half hour later, he was in his car on the way to the restaurant. Pulling into the parking lot, he noticed that Janelle had just arrived and was walking toward the door. Pushing his worries back, he steeled himself and got out of the car, meeting Janelle by the door. "You weren't waiting, were you?"

Love Means ... *Courage*

"Oh, no." She smiled as he held the door for her. "I just got here."

"Good." He took her jacket, and one of the waitresses led them to a table. The restaurant wasn't fancy, just a small family-style restaurant, but the food was good and plentiful.

"Hey, Janelle, Len, what can I get for you?"

"Hi, Lacy." Len said as he looked to Janelle to let her order first. "How are things going?"

"Not bad." Her smile faded just a little. "I heard about your job. You'll find something better, I know it." Len remembered Lacy from one of his early college classes. She hadn't done well and had given up after a semester, but she always had a smile and never seemed to let things get her down. Len had to admire that.

"Thanks." Len watched the surprised look on Janelle's face along with something else he couldn't quite read.

Janelle put down her menu. "I'll have the fish special and a Diet Coke."

"And I'll have a burger and fries." Lacy gave him another smile, and then she went to place the order.

"What happened, Len?"

"Business has been slow, and they needed to cut back. I was the last one hired, so they let me go." He shrugged and tried to stay positive, while at the same time marveling just how quickly news spread in town. "On Monday, I'll start looking for another job." He tried to sound casual. "Don't worry about it. How have you been?"

She started telling him a whole litany of things that had happened in the last week. "I got a job at the telephone company in customer service and billing. I start Monday." She was so excited, and Len did his best to be happy for her. It certainly wasn't her fault that he'd been laid off, and she had every right to be excited. "When Papa died, he left me his life insurance money, but I've wanted to save it for emergencies, and now with my own job, I can be fully independent," Janelle explained. Their conversation quieted as their food arrived, but as soon as Lacy left, Janelle picked up where she left off.

Len listened and smiled as she told him all about her new job, the woman barely stopping to take a breath or eat, she was so happy. When her father had died, she'd taken it quite hard and even moved out of the family home to live with an aunt. Len finished his dinner and listened as Janelle talked.

"Say, Len, I just had an idea." She'd finished eating and was sipping her coffee. "My brother could use some help on the farm. He's short-handed and needs people he can rely on."

"I don't know anything about farming." Len wasn't sure this was a good fit for him. "I've worked with horses, and I can ride, but doesn't your brother raise cattle?

"Yes, so…?"

"I don't know the first thing about cows."

She laughed after she sipped her coffee. "You don't really need to." She put down her cup and looked seriously at Len. "Ever since Ruby and my dad died, he's had a difficult time of it, what with the farm and trying to raise a baby on his own. He needs some help, and you need a job." When she said it like that, it seemed so reasonable.

"What could I do to help him?"

She shook her head and looked exasperated. "If you're not interested, fine, but I thought you might need a job."

Love Means ... *Courage*

Len smiled and tried to diffuse the tension that had suddenly crept in. "Maybe you're right. It wouldn't hurt for me to talk to him."

"Excellent!" Her smile was radiant, and Len realized he'd been coerced into doing exactly what she'd wanted. Hell, if he didn't know better, he'd think they were dating. "I'll call Cliff tonight and tell him you'll be by to see him." They finished their coffee, and Len asked for the check.

After paying, they left the restaurant, and he walked Janelle to her car. "Thank you. I'll stop by and see Cliff tomorrow. Who knows, maybe I can help him." He held the car door for her as she got in the car, closing it behind her with a thunk. She started the car and waved as she pulled away. Walking across the small lot, he got in his own car and headed home.

Pulling into the yard, he parked next to his mother's car and went inside. As he expected, she was sitting in the living room watching television. "How was dinner?"

"Good." He sat on the sofa. "Janelle told me that her brother is looking for some help on the farm and asked me to go over tomorrow and talk to him." She turned her head, looking skeptical, but said nothing. "It's a job, and I could sure use the money, at least until something else comes along."

"Well, it certainly can't hurt to talk to him."

Len wasn't so sure that was true. He hadn't seen Cliff since Ruby died. She had invited him to dinner a number of times, and each time, Cliff had been polite but distant. If he were honest with himself, he wasn't so sure Cliff would want him to work at the farm, and he wasn't so sure *he* wanted to work there. Every time he saw Cliff, the first thing that sprang to mind was that night, that second behind the barn when he'd felt Cliff's lips next to his. He knew he shouldn't, but he just couldn't help it. Cliff Laughton had been the star of his feverish imagination even before that kiss, and to be so close to him on a daily basis—

"Len!"

He heard his name and jerked himself back to the present. "Sorry, Mom. What were you saying?"

"I was asking you if Janelle told you what time you should be there?"

"No. She didn't mention a specific time, but I'll go over in the morning." He had to keep his mind from wandering all the time. Cliff had married Ruby. Whatever had happened in high school was a long time ago. Besides, Cliff had probably just gotten swept up in the moment and had regretted what he'd done as soon as it was over. "I'm going to clean up and go to bed." He lifted himself from the old sofa and headed to his small room.

Len grabbed some sweatpants and a T-shirt and went across the small hall to the bathroom. Stripping off his clothes, he started the shower and climbed beneath the spray. The hot water felt good and washed away much of the day's tension, and there seemed to be plenty of it. As he started to relax, he felt parts of him begin to stiffen. It had been a while since… well, since he'd allowed himself any sort of release, and his body was definitely ready. Slowly, he ran his hands down his stomach, sliding them along his length. He wanted to moan, but he bit it back; the walls were paper thin. So he clamped his mouth shut and continued to stroke, letting his mind wander. It didn't take long before a vision came to his mind: a face with deep eyes and thick brown hair and lips that just begged to be kissed. "Cliff." The word escaped his lips before he could stop it.

Forcing the image from his mind, he tried to concentrate on something else, someone else, anyone else, but it wasn't working, and things started going downhill from there. His mind wouldn't cooperate and neither would the shower, because the water started going cold.

Love Means ... *Courage*

He was just getting out of the shower when he heard his mother call. Putting a towel around his waist, he cracked open the door. "Yes?" He heard her on the phone, and then she hung up.

"That was Janelle. She said to stop by Cliff's in the morning but not too early." That was really strange. Farmers were early risers; they had to be in order to get the work done while they had the sun.

"Okay. Thank you." He closed the door and finished drying off before hanging up his towel and putting on the sweats and T-shirt. After making sure he'd left the bathroom clean—his mother had trained him well—he went out and found his mom still in the living room. Saying good night, he went to his room and climbed into bed.

Chapter 4

LEN pulled up in front of the Laughton family farm at about nine in the morning, thinking that wasn't early by farm standards, and parked near the barn where he saw a few other vehicles. No one seemed to be around, but he heard a tractor and other equipment in the distance and figured that the other men were already working. Walking across the yard, he noticed how different things were from his last visit, before Ruby died. "Jesus, what in the hell is wrong?" Even to his eyes, things didn't look right at all.

The yard around the house hadn't been mowed in what must have been weeks; the grass was so tall. The buildings looked in good shape, but the rest of the place looked a little neglected. Walking along the path, he knocked on the kitchen door and waited. After a few minutes, he knocked again. Finally, he heard footsteps inside and the door opened.

"Yeah."

"Cliff, it's Len Parker. Janelle said I should come by. She said you needed some help." Cliff looked terrible: dark circles under his eyes, drawn complexion, sallow skin. Nothing like the man Len remembered.

Love Means ... *Courage*

"Oh, yeah." Cliff ran his fingers through his long, shaggy hair. "Come on in." He moved to open the door farther but stopped, and Len saw a pair of eyes and a head of light hair peek out from behind his legs.

"I'm Len, and you must be Geoff." The little boy stuck his thumb in his mouth and nodded before hiding again. Cliff picked up the little boy, who was still in his pajamas, and then opened the door wide enough to let Len inside.

The kitchen was a mess: dishes in the sink and stuff all over the table. It wasn't particularly dirty, just a cluttered mess, like Cliff didn't know what to do with everything. *What the hell was wrong with the man?* He led Len through to the living room, which wasn't much better than the kitchen, except this room was filled with toys of every description, all over everything. "Sorry about the mess." He moved the toys off one of the chairs and sat down. Len did the same. "So, Len, how have you been?"

"So-so. I was working at the Ford dealership until yesterday." He handed Cliff his letter of recommendation. "Janelle said you needed some help."

"I do. I lost the man who ran the barn a few weeks ago and haven't been able to find anyone."

More like haven't had the gumption to look. Len kept that to himself, although he desperately wanted to say it. "I've worked with horses, and I can ride. Growing up I didn't have the money for riding lessons, so I worked for them." *Worked hard too.*

He waited to see what Cliff was going to say, but the man just sat back in the chair with Geoff spread over his body, holding tight to the little boy. The man was lost, completely lost. Len could see that, but it wasn't his place to say anything, so he waited.

"Can you start today? Pay's two hundred a week." *About what I was making at the car dealership.*

"Sure." Len smiled and watched as the youngster lifted his head off his dad's shoulders and looked over at Len before squirming to get down. He stood at his father's feet for a minute before walking over to Len. "He looks just like his mother." The words were out of his mouth before he could stop them, and he wanted to kick himself.

But all Cliff said was a simple, "Yes, he does," and then he clammed up. This man was so different from the outgoing, take-on-the-world Cliff he'd known before Ruby died.

"Well, I'll get started then." He'd worn work clothes just in case.

He stood up, and Geoff stepped back, looking up at him. "You taw." It came out sounding like "Utah," but Len understood and knelt down in front of the toddler.

"You'll be tall soon too." After ruffling the kid's hair, he stood back up and headed outside. He stopped at his car and got a hat before heading to the barn. He took one step inside and recoiled at the smell. "Jesus Christ!" He pushed open the doors and let in some light and air before walking through. Four heads peered out of stalls, and he introduced himself to each one.

There appeared to be twelve stalls total: four occupied, four others that appeared dirty, and four empty. It looked to Len like they'd simply moved the horses instead of cleaning their stalls. "Jesus H. Christ, what a mess." He continued walking through the barn and opened the tack room. Inside was a jumbled mess with half the tack on the floor. "Looks like I've got my work cut out for me."

Behind the last stall, Len found a wheelbarrow, a shovel, and a pitchfork. Digging in, he began cleaning out the worst of the stalls, shoveling the soiled bedding into the wheelbarrow and hauling it to what appeared to be the muck pile. Back and forth he went for hours, hauling out the muck and carrying in fresh sawdust.

Love Means ... *Courage*

By noon, he had four stalls ready, and the horses were resettled in clean stalls with fresh hay and water.

He walked to his car and got out the cooler with his lunch and sat in the shade to eat. The late April warmth was nice. A great day for working, not too hot and not too cold. He sat, ate, and watched the house. There hadn't been any sign of Cliff or anyone else all morning.

After finishing his lunch, he went back to work, cleaning out the remaining four stalls and then sweeping down the barn. By the time he was done, the barn smelled fresh and clean.

He checked his watch. It was just after three, so he went into the tack room and began ripping it apart, getting all the loose and jumbled items pulled out. Then he began putting them back and organizing them. "What a job. It looks like nobody's done anything in here for months."

"Close enough."

Len jumped at the voice and turned around to see a tall, slim man leaning against the door frame. "Sorry, I didn't know anyone was there. I'm Len Parker." He held out his hand.

"Fred Jenkins." The two men shook hands. "I take it Cliff hired you."

"Yeah, he said the man who took care of the barn quit."

Fred smiled a huge smile that wasn't completely pleasant. "He didn't quit; we run him off, the lazy, good-for-nothing loafer." Len wondered if he needed to be worried. "You got more work done in here in a day that he did in a week." Now the smile changed and became much more genuine.

"Well, I'm almost done here. The tack's nearly organized, and the stalls are cleaned. I just got to get some hay down from the loft and make sure the horses are set for the night, and I'll be ready to call it a day."

"I'll help you get the hay down. We need to make sure the oldest is used first."

Len nodded and smiled before turning around and finishing up the tack room. When he was done, the room was swept, organized, and clean. Closing the door behind him, he saw Fred watering the horses.

"Thought I'd help. You ready to get the hay?" Fred led him upstairs, and Len whistled as he saw the nearly full loft. "We used to have a lot more horses, but when Cliff's dad died and with that ass Holder running the barn, most of the boarders left." He shook his head and led Len around to the back of the barn where the back quarter of the loft was empty. "This is the oldest, not that it's that old, but we need to use it first." He raised a trap door in the loft, and they started throwing down bales.

"What's going on here? I haven't seen Cliff all day."

Fred shook his head and shrugged before grabbing another bale and dropping it through the hole. "Wish I knew. None of us does. We're all doing the best we can."

"What time does everyone get here in the morning?"

"Most of us are here at seven, but we need to be quiet because of Geoff."

Somehow Len doubted that was really the reason. He'd noticed all the beer cans in the kitchen trash, and he knew the circles under Cliff's eyes weren't only from lack of sleep, but he didn't say anything to Fred.

"Sundays are a quick day, feed the horses, and take care of anything pressing. We try to leave at noon."

Love Means ... *Courage*

"Hey, Fred!" A new voice called from outside the barn.

"In here, Randy!"

A huge, barrel-shaped man lumbered into the barn. "Hey." He stopped when he saw Len, but it was the clean barn smell that really got him. "You the guy replacing Holder?"

Len nodded and actually heard Randy inhale.

"Damn, I love the smell of a clean barn." The big man held out his hand, "Randy Marsh."

"Len Parker." They shook hands, Randy's paw dwarfing Len's as he gripped it.

"You do all this today?" Len smiled and nodded, liking that he'd made a good impression. "You'll do just fine."

"Does anyone else work here, or is it just the two... I mean three of us?"

"It's just us." Randy squinted like he was trying to remember something. "I've seen you around here before."

"I knew Ruby. She and I were...." He swallowed. "...close friends, had been since high school." As a group they all nodded slowly.

Randy tilted his head in the direction of the house. "He ain't been the same since she passed."

"I knew Cliff in school, and he's nothing like he was then." Len almost said more but stopped himself. They didn't need to be gossiping about their boss, even if they all seemed to feel for him. "So how do things work around here?"

They two men looked at each other before Fred answered. "When Carter was alive, we'd meet every morning and discuss what needed to be done. He'd hand out assignments, and we'd get to work, but lately we've been on our own, so we just get to work."

"Do you mind if we get together tomorrow morning?" Len looked around the barn. "Taking care of things in here isn't a full-time job, and I can help with other things if you're willing to work with me."

Both men looked at each other and eventually nodded. "We won't say no to the help," Randy said as he turned and left the barn with Fred right behind him. "We'll see you at seven tomorrow."

Len got back to work, filling the mangers with fresh hay and greeting each horse with a stroke on the nose as their heads appeared. "Would you guys like some treats?" Majestic heads bobbed as though they understood what he was saying. "I'll bring you some carrots tomorrow." After a final check of the barn, he closed the door and walked across the hayfield that passed for a yard.

Approaching the house, he saw the back door open. A tiny foot lowered itself onto the step, and then a small body slipped around the door.

He called the toddler's name, not wanting him to fall. "Geoff."

"Wen…." Geoff pointed to the barn. "Hos, hos." He turned around and then lowered himself down the next step and onto the ground before running through the tall grass toward the barn as fast as his legs would carry him. "Hos, hos."

Len scooped the youngster into his arms. "You want to go see the horses?" Geoff's little head nodded violently. Len looked back at the quiet house and wondered again what was going on but decided it couldn't hurt to let Geoff see the horses. "Who dressed you, little man?" Geoff was still wearing his pajama bottoms, but he'd pulled off the top and was just wearing his undershirt and a pair of blue socks with no shoes.

"Me." He seemed so proud of himself.

"Okay, let's go see the horses." He bounced the little boy in his arms, giggles, squeals, and laughs accompanying them as they walked to the barn. Len opened the barn door, and large heads appeared, looking at their visitors.

"Hos, hos." Geoff's little hand pointed at the nearest head.

"Let's go see Misty; she's really nice." She'd appeared to be the most docile when he'd moved her to clean her stall. Len lifted Geoff, holding him where Misty could see him. His little hand stroked her nose.

"Nice hos, nice hos," Geoff chanted in his small voice, as he stroked Misty's long nose.

"Geoff!" He heard Cliff's voice carry into the barn, sounding a little panicked. "Geoff, where are you?"

"We're in here, Cliff. He's fine." Heavy footsteps came up behind them as he held Geoff so he could stroke the horse.

"Hos, daddy, hos." The delight in Geoff's voice rang through the barn. "Hos, hos, hos."

Len looked over at Cliff and saw the worry and panic begin to fade. Cliff stepped close, and Len handed Geoff over to his father. "I found him climbing out the back door heading toward the barn."

"Thank you." Len nodded slightly and watched as Geoff leaned toward Misty, trying to reach her again. "We should go back inside and get you ready for dinner."

Cliff began to walk out of the barn. "Hos, daddy, hoooosssss."

"I know; you can see them again tomorrow." A glint of happiness crossed Cliff's face as he talked to Geoff.

"Pwomise?" Cliff's response died away as they left the barn.

Len patted Misty on the nose and left the barn as well, closing the door behind him and heading to his car. He opened the door and collapsed into the seat. "Fuck, I'm tired." He started the car and pulled out of the drive, heading for home. The drive home was almost automatic, and he pulled into the yard and half stumbled into the house.

"I take it you got the job?"

"Yeah, I got it all right." He collapsed into one of the kitchen chairs, resting his head on the table. "Barn looked like it hadn't been touched in weeks. The entire place looks sort of neglected."

"Doesn't he have enough help?" Len's mom stood at the stove, making dinner.

"Don't know, Mom. But I didn't see him all day. Just stayed in his house." Len didn't mention the things he suspected. "I met the guys. They seem nice enough, and they're concerned about him too." He let his voice trail off.

"Do you want to help him?" She began dishing up plates, and he pushed himself up and got the silverware and glasses, forcing his cramping legs to move.

"I don't know what I can do."

"Do a good job, and be a friend when he needs one, even if he doesn't realize he needs it."

"How'd you get to be so smart?" She put his plate in front of him, and he looked up at her. "Can we really afford steak?"

"It was on sale, and besides, you're going to need your strength." That was a definite. He cut into his meat and raised the fork to his mouth. As soon as that first bite hit his tongue, his ravenous hunger took over, and he wolfed down his meal.

Love Means ... *Courage*

"Thanks, Mom. That was delicious." He put his plate in the sink and sat back down to keep her company while she finished eating.

"Go get cleaned up and rest. Do you work tomorrow?"

He made a quick mental note to call Janelle and let her know he got the job. "Only till noon or so." He lifted himself off the chair and dragged himself into the bathroom where he started the shower.

A half hour later, clean and relaxed, he sat in the living room watching television, but soon he found himself falling asleep, so he said good night and headed to bed, immediately falling into a near comatose sleep that he didn't wake from until his alarm blared in his ears.

CHAPTER 5

THE sun was sending its first rays of light over the trees as he arrived at the farm. Everything was quiet and still. Len coasted into the same parking space he'd used the day before and got out of his car, closing the door softly. The chill in the morning air hit his skin as he walked across the gravel drive to the barn.

"Morning, sunshines!" He flipped on the light and was greeted by sleepy heads poking out of their stalls. A few of them actually had the nerve to yawn. "That's enough of that; I've got work to do." Len walked to the spigot and got fresh water, filling each of their troughs before adding hay to their mangers. "I'll let you eat for a while, but then you're all going outside." He liked talking to the horses, and they seemed to respond to his voice. He grabbed the broom and swept the walk and the empty stalls.

"Well, what do we have here?" Len knelt down and found a mother and her newborn kittens curled beneath one of the empty mangers. She tensed, and Len backed away and left her alone.

Opening the doors to the pastures, he made sure there was water in the pasture troughs and let the horses out for some exercise, giving each of them one of the carrots his mother had sent along before letting them run. With the barn to himself, he grabbed the wheelbarrow and spot-cleaned the stalls, scooping out the messed parts and replacing them with fresh sawdust. He was just finishing when he heard a vehicle pull into the drive. Putting away the broom, he left the barn to see both Fred and Randy walking toward the barn.

"You're here early."

"Yeah. Got the horses out in the pastures and the barn cleaned for the day." Len leaned against one of the empty stall doors.

Fred sat on a hay bale. "We've got to check on the cattle. There are a few fences that need checking, and it's supposed to rain this afternoon."

"You guys need any help?"

"Naw, we got it. Shouldn't take us very long. What have you got in mind for today?"

"There're a few breaks in the riding ring fence I'd like to get fixed. I was going to ask Cliff to advertise that we have stall space and a riding ring so we could attract some boarders, but the ring's not usable as it is now." Len looked out the barn door to the yard. "And I was thinking I'd try to clean up the mess out front. Can't attract anybody with the place looking so shabby." Len walked to the door looking out over the yard.

Randy stood next to him. "Don't go makin' noise too early, Cliff'll ream you a new one if you wake Geoff." Len looked over toward the house and saw the back door open, a small face peering out the screen door before pushing on it, trying to get out.

"I don't think waking Geoff is something we need to worry about." Len pointed to the back door. "I think it's Cliff who wants to sleep in. Probably sleeping off what he was drinking last night." There he went, shooting his mouth off when he should know to keep quiet.

Randy looked doubtful. "We ain't never seen him drinkin'."

In for a penny, in for a pound. "When I was in the kitchen yesterday, the trash was full of beer cans. Looked to me like he was taking most of his meals in liquid form." Len looked at the other two. "Maybe I should have kept my mouth shut."

"What are we gonna do?"

Len looked at Fred, smiling in surprise. "One thing we're gonna do is stop pandering to him. This is a farm, and work needs to get done, so we're gonna do it. You guys go ahead and get started."

"But we need the tractor to...." Randy stopped and smiled wide. "I get it. Okay, I'm in. Let's wake him up." Randy walked to the equipment shed and climbed onto the tractor, starting the huge machine. Fred climbed on and the two of them got to work, driving it out the drive before turning down the road. As the sound faded in the distance, Len went to the equipment shed and found a riding lawn mower. Climbing on, he turned the key and the engine turned over. Putting it in gear, he pulled it out and rode to the yard before engaging the mower and starting the yard cleanup.

The sun was shining brightly as he mowed swathes of the backyard. "Hey!" He heard someone calling. He disengaged the mower and turned down the engine. "Len, what are you doing at this hour?" He looked up and saw one of the bedroom windows open, Cliff leaning out.

"I'm mowing the hay field you call a yard, what does it look like I'm doing?" Len didn't wait for a response. He turned up the engine and engaged the mower deck, drowning out whatever Cliff yelled down at him.

Len continued mowing, finishing the backyard and starting on the front. As he approached the house, he could see Geoff standing in the living room window, his face plastered to the glass, his little hand waving. Len chuckled and waved, watching as Geoff began to jump up and down. He could just imagine the squeals ringing through the house. When he made his next pass, Geoff was gone, and Len finished up the yard and started mowing the patches of grass near and around the barns before driving the mover back into the shed and turning it off.

"What the hell are you doing?" Cliff came charging across the yard with Geoff in his arms. "You woke him up with all that racket!"

"Woke *you* up, more like." Len stared at Cliff, meeting the man's eyes, challenging him because he knew Cliff was lying. "I saw Geoff running around the living room before I even started. I think the only person I woke was you, and it looks to me like you need to wake the hell up!"

"Where do you get off telling me anything?" Geoff began to whimper, and Cliff lowered his voice. "Last time I looked, this was my farm." His words were forced out between gritted teeth.

"Then act like it, Cliff. Your men are doing their best to hold this place together, but they need guidance. Hell, look around you. Your barn's empty instead of filled with revenue-producing horses. Your loft is full of hay that the horses you have couldn't eat in three years, with more in the field that will need to be cut. Your yard looked like a hay field, making the entire place look shabby. The stalls in the barn hadn't been cleaned in weeks."

"The barn's what I hired you for. If you can't handle it—"

"Don't be an ass! The barn's cleaned, the tack room organized, your horses in the pasture, and your yard's been mowed. I can more than handle it. Can you?" Len glared at his boss, not willing to back down. But he couldn't keep from noticing how fiery Cliff's eyes were, or how his lips looked so full and kissable when he was angry, and damn, he wanted to feel them again. He felt his expression start to soften, and then he remembered that there was no way it was going to happen, and he let his frustration steel his gaze.

"Wen, hos, hos." Geoff began squirming to get down, and Cliff turned around heading toward the house. Geoff let out a bloodcurdling wail. "Wen hos! Hos!" Cliff turned around, shoving Geoff into Len's arms before stalking back to the house, growling under his breath.

Len waited until he was almost at the door. "Enjoy your beer!" Cliff stopped for a second, and then he disappeared in the house, slamming the door hard enough to rattle the windows.

Len turned to look at Geoff; the boy's eyes were huge. "Cwiff ass." He then started to giggle like he'd said the funniest thing in the world. "Cwiff ass." He laughed again and pointed to the barn. "Hos."

"Okay, let's go see the horses." He walked to the pasture, carrying Geoff, who, like the day before, was still in his pajamas, but at least they were different ones. "See, they're outside, running and playing." Geoff watched the horses and tried to call them over, but they were happy to be outside and continued their grazing. "Well," he looked back at the house, wondering if Cliff was going to come get his son. "Looks like you are gonna help me with chores." He bounced the toddler in his arms, earning high-pitched laughs and squeals. "Let's see what we can find to do."

Around the side of the barn he found a tractor tire. Sitting where Len put him near the ring, the youngster watched as Len rolled the tire to a safe spot away from the ring. He also found some sand that looked like it was left from a building project of some type, and he filled the tire. "There, how's that for a sandbox?" Geoff raced over, climbed onto the tire, and started digging with his hands. "We need to get you some toys." Picking Geoff out of the sandbox, he carried him back to the house and opened the back door.

"Cliff?" No response. Len figured he was upstairs and walked through the kitchen to the living room. "Let's get you some sandbox toys." In one corner behind a chair, he found a pail and shovel. With

Love Means ... *Courage*

Geoff's help, he filled it with cars and trucks. "Cliff, I've got Geoff, and we'll be out by the ring." Still no response. Shit, maybe he'd pushed too hard, but damn if the man hadn't needed it. "Let's go play in the sand."

"Daddy, sand!"

"You wanna go play?"

Geoff ran to the window and pointed. "Wen hos."

"Let's go then." Picking him up again, Len, looked around the still house one more time before carrying Geoff back outside and out to the riding ring. Placing him in the makeshift sandbox, he gave him his toys, and Geoff immediately went to work, digging to China.

With Geoff occupied, Len began surveying the fencing around the ring. The posts seemed solid enough, but some of the cross braces needed repair, and the ring was full of weeds. Needing to keep an eye on Geoff, he started with the weeding. He spent the next hour of so on his hands and knees, pulling the tall, errant plants. They came up easily, and he was able to get the ring looking pretty decent. Geoff continued playing in the sand, having a jolly old time.

"Hey, Geoffy, you making a sand castle?" Len called as he watched Geoff play. Geoff didn't even lift his head, he was so engrossed. And Len continued with his work.

"Having fun, Geoffy?" There was no trace of his earlier anger in Cliff's voice.

"Hi, Daddy!" Len looked up from his weeding and saw Cliff bending down near the sandbox, father and son talking while Geoff continued digging and running his cars on sand highways.

Len watched for a minute and then went back to work, pulling the last of the weeds. As he worked, he still found himself looking toward the sandbox, but now, instead of watching Geoff, he found himself watching Cliff. The way his body moved, the way he played with his son, the way his jeans tightened over his thighs when he knelt down. *I can't be doing this to myself.* Cliff turned to look at him, and Len put his head back down, concentrating on what he was doing. When he lifted his head again, he saw Cliff looking back at him. Busted. He covered as best he could by pretending to look at Geoff and then returning his attention to the weeding.

A few seconds later, he heard footsteps approach and stop next to him. Pulling the last of the weeds, he lifted his eyes, staring right into the crook of Cliff's crouched legs. "Looking good, Len."

He wasn't kidding; from what Len could see, it looked real good. Thick legs and…. Len swallowed and forced himself to look up, hoping he wasn't turning red. He forced his attention away from Cliff and back on work. "Thanks." He dumped the last of the weeds into a bushel basket and then sat up. "I was going to repair the fencing, but I wasn't sure where to find the supplies."

Len watched as Cliff looked over at Geoff. "I think you'll find what you need in the equipment shed." Len barely heard what Cliff said, his attention wandering. Oh, he heard the words, and his brain registered the idea, but his eyes saw Cliff's lips moving, and his brain short-circuited.

"You okay?" He felt Cliff's hand on his shoulder, the warmth seeping through his shirt.

"Yeah, sorry." Len glanced at his watch to cover his embarrassment. "I'll go see what I can find." Cliff stood back up, and Len watched his legs flex out of the corner of his eye. And unfortunately, he felt his pants grow tighter. Cliff walked back toward where Geoff was playing, and Len used the opportunity to walk to the equipment shed. There were indeed a few cross braces he could use, and he carried them back to the ring, returning to get the tool kit.

Love Means ... *Courage*

Cliff looked up from where he and Geoff were playing. "You need some help?"

"Won't turn you down." He set down the tool kit and got a hammer to pry off the broken pieces.

Len heard Cliff tell Geoff to stay in the sandbox.

"Okay, Daddy." Geoff didn't even look up from the hole he was digging, and Len smiled to himself as he finished prying off the remnants of the broken cross brace. Cliff picked up the new brace and held it in place while Len attached it with long nails.

They worked together in companionable quiet, talking only when they needed something. There were so many things Len wanted to ask, but it just wasn't any of his business, and Cliff was his boss. What he really wanted to know right then, more than anything else, was why he got this fluttery feeling in his stomach every time he got near Cliff. He'd felt it when he was in the house with him yesterday, and he could feel it again now. He really wished he could ask Tim about it, but his friend was already gone, and he didn't know anyone else to ask.

A voice echoed through the barn. "Hey, Len, you need any help?"

He turned and called, "We're out back in the ring."

Fred and Randy stepped out of the barn and strode into the ring. "We're finished with the cattle and were wondering if you needed any help." They both seemed to see Cliff at the same time. "Hey, Boss."

"Hey, guys." Cliff walked to them while Len sank the last nail. "Everything okay?"

Fred answered, "Seems to be for now. The cattle are fed and watered. We checked fences this week, and they held up pretty well over the winter, but there are some weak areas we need to fix. We'll get to them this week."

"Anything else?" Fred shook his head slowly, and Cliff turned his attention to Geoff, still playing in the sandbox. "Then why don't you take off and enjoy the rest of the day."

They turned and disappeared into the barn, only to reappear a few seconds later, walking up to Len. "We're going to Steve's for lunch; you wanna join us?"

"Sure, I just need to put things away and get the horses in." He looked at the cloudy spring sky. "Looks like rain."

"We'll start with the horses and meet you out front in a few minutes."

Len gathered up the tools and stopped by the sandbox, watching as Cliff helped Geoff put away his toys, which the toddler was none too happy about. "I wanna play, Daddy."

"I know, but it's going to rain. You can play inside." The toys in the pail, Cliff picked up Geoff and the toys and started walking through the barn, Len following behind, carrying the tools.

"Hos, daddy, hos." Cliff stiffened and looked like he was becoming impatient.

"Geoff, tomorrow if it's nice, I'll take you for a ride on a horse, but only if you're good for your daddy." Len's voice exuded patience.

Those big eyes widened, and that face broke into an adorable smile. "Okay, Wen." His little hand waved good-bye as Cliff carried him toward the house. Len waved back and then let the horses into the barn, settling them in their stalls as the first drops of rain fell on the roof.

Love Means ... *Courage*

Randy and Fred were waiting for him as he finished. "You can ride with us, and we'll bring you back here." Len nodded, and they all headed for Fred's truck. The ride to Scottville didn't take long, but it was pouring by the time they parked and got out of the truck. They hurried inside and sat at one of the few empty tables.

"Hi, guys."

Randy blushed as he said hello. "Hi Shell."

She handed them menus. "What can I get you to drink?" Fred ordered a beer, with Randy and Len following suit. "Coming right up. You know what you want to eat?" She stood near Randy, leaning in close. "I can come back if you don't."

"Could you give us just a minute?"

"Sure, darling." She winked at Randy and then hurried to another table.

"See, Randy?" Fred sipped his water. "I told you she's flirting with you." Len watched as both men looked to where Shell was waiting on another table, standing tall.

"She's just doing that to get better tips."

Fred smirked. "She didn't do it with me or Len, and she's not doing it with them either—just you. So be a man and ask her out, for Pete's sake." They looked at their menus, and Len saw Randy become more nervous.

"You boys know what you want?" She again stood right next to Randy, practically touching his arm with her hip. If she were any more obvious, she'd have to have been sitting in his lap. Len and Fred ordered, and she turned her attention to Randy. "What're you having, sugar?"

"Umm, your phone number? I mean…." The man stammered helplessly. "I was wondering if I could call you. Maybe take you out?"

She leaned down and wrote on his napkin. "I'd love to, sugar." When Randy stopped gaping like a big-mouth bass, he smiled and placed his order. She smiled back at him and walked away, being sure he was watching.

Fred clapped Randy on the back. "Way to go."

Shell brought their beers a few minutes later. "Here you go." She smiled at Randy and turned to leave but then came back. "You still work out at the Laughton farm, don't you?"

"Yeah," Fred said as he motioned across the table, "and Len just started this week."

Shell looked around and then leaned in dramatically. "You know this place is gossip central, and I don't place much faith in it, but I've been hearing that he may be having some money troubles. Don't know if it's true, but I overheard some guys talking yesterday." She straightened up. "I'll be right back with your food."

All three of them stared at her as she retreated, wondering if it could be true. "Should we start looking for new jobs?"

"Whoa, Randy. That's just idle gossip. If Cliff was having problems, he would have told us. Wouldn't he?" Fred's gaze shifted from Randy to Len, who just shrugged.

Len spoke up. "Don't worry about it now. It's probably just gossip. Besides, Randy got himself a date, or at least her phone number." The lightness returned to the conversation as they raised their glasses and toasted Randy. Their food arrived, and they started eating. Well, Len and Fred started eating. Randy talked to Shell, and they made a date for next Saturday night.

Love Means ... *Courage*

It was still raining when they paid the bill and left the restaurant. A quick dash to the truck, and they all climbed inside. Fred turned on the radio, and they heard the end of Steve Perry's *Oh Sherrie* and then the news. The reporter droned on, and Fred sped up when they reported a barn fire but relaxed when it wasn't Cliff's.

They arrived at the farm, and Len made a run into the barn while Randy raced to his truck, and then both vehicles crunched down the drive.

The barn was quiet, and Len peered into each stall occupied, making sure the occupants were settled and happy. He was about to leave when he heard the door open and close. Turning, he saw Cliff and Geoff under a huge umbrella. Geoff squirmed to get down and ran to the nearest stall. "Hos." His little blue-jeaned legs were going ninety to nothing.

"He has a one-track mind." Cliff let him go.

"That he does." Len walked to the toddler, who at that moment was jumping up and down, trying to reach the horse. "You want to give him a treat?" The small body stilled, and he turned and smiled. "Yes!"

"Yes, what?" The scolding was mild.

"Yes, pwease!" Len picked him up and handed Geoff a carrot from the bag he'd brought that morning, and the boy immediately put it in his own mouth.

"That's for the horse." Geoff took it out of his mouth and held out his hand, giggling as the horse took the carrot, its lips sliding over his tiny palm.

"More, Wen." Geoff insisted on giving each horse a carrot, tasting them all first. Len held him as he fed each horse. Len peeked over at Cliff, making sure he was okay with this, and the look on his face nearly stopped Len in his tracks. His face was relaxed, soft, with a gentle smile and sparkling eyes—the Cliff he remembered. Len felt the flippity-flop in his stomach start up again. As soon as Len put the toddler down, Geoff raced back to his dad, laughing and clinging to his legs.

"I should be getting home." He packed up the carrots and put them in the tack room. When he got back, Cliff had the umbrella up and Geoff in his arms. "I'll see you in the morning," Len called as he raced to his car.

CHAPTER 6

"THE commerce department reported yesterday that failures of family-owned farms reached their highest level since the Great Depression." Len turned off the radio as he drove. That type of news he didn't need.

It was still dark when he arrived back at the farm the following morning. Everything was still wet from the rain, but the clouds were gone, and the spring sun would dry everything pretty fast. He let the horses out into the pastures and spot-cleaned the stalls. He was just finishing up when he heard the phone ring. Figuring it rang both in the barn and at the house, he answered it. "Laughton Farms. Can I help you?"

"Oh, thank goodness." The woman on the line sounded frazzled. "I was wondering if you board horses."

"Yes, we do, and we have space available." Len could hear her breathing a sigh of relief. "We have an outdoor ring as well as lush pastures."

"What are your rates?" Len had no idea and began looking around the tack room to see if there was anything. He found a sheet that listed rates from 1982. He figured they were in the ballpark, but added twenty-five dollars just in case.

"It's a hundred and seventy-five dollars a month." He tried to remember the terms at the barn from when he was taking lessons. "First and last month paid in advance. That includes the stall, hay and oats, as well as time in the pasture if you request it." He ticked the items off on his fingers. "Vet fees, supplements, and any special requirements are extra."

"How often are the stalls cleaned?" The anxiety was gone from her voice, and she was now all business.

"Minimum of once a week, with spot-cleaning daily. I like a clean barn."

"I'm a trainer as well. Would you have any objection to me using your facilities for lessons?"

"Of course not."

"Could you hold on a minute?"

"Certainly." He could hear her covering the phone with her hand, and he waited for her to come back on the line. "Could you take five horses?"

"Five?" That was a huge surprise. "Yes, we have room. May I ask what happened?"

"The barn we were using was hit by lightning. We were able to get the horses out but not much else. If it's not a problem, we'll load the horses and bring them over in the next hour or so." Len could barely believe his ears. He hoped Cliff would be pleased. "My name is Nicole Robinson, and I'll see you soon."

"I'm Len, the barn manager, and I'll be looking for you." He hung up the phone and started for the door. Jesus, he hoped he'd done the right thing. After all, the barn was empty, and Cliff had

Love Means ... *Courage*

hired him to manage the barn, so he had. Len left the tack room and got to work. The stalls that weren't being used were bare, so he got busy hauling loads of sawdust for bedding.

"Morning, Len."

"Morning, Fred." He dumped the load and spread the bedding, closing the stall door.

"You're busy this morning. What's up?"

"Do you know a Nicole Robinson, by any chance?"

Fred chuckled. "Sure, everyone that has anything to do with horses knows Nicole. She's one of the best riding instructors in the county. Trains out at Old Man Padgett's place. Why?"

"That barn that burned yesterday must have been Old Man Padgett's, because she's on her way over with five horses." Len smiled as the business student in him took over.

"Does Cliff know?"

Len shook his head. "I just got off the phone with her, and I've got four more stalls to get ready before she gets here."

Fred grabbed the wheelbarrow. "I'll haul; you spread and get the stalls finished. Randy will be here in a few minutes, and he can check on the cattle."

They heard Randy's truck pull up, and Len told him the plan while Fred began hauling. Len returned to the barn, and a few minutes later the tractor started, and Randy headed out. They worked like men possessed, preparing five stalls with bedding, hay, water, and a little grain. They were just finishing up when they heard tires on the gravel drive and then the crunch of feet.

Len closed the last stall door and walked out front to near pandemonium. There were three horse trailers. "People, please."

Everyone looked at Len. "Which of you is Nicole?" A middle-aged, stocky woman stepped forward, and Len introduced himself, shaking her hand. "What seems to be the problem?"

"After I hung up with you, some more owners arrived, and they followed us over, hoping you might have stalls." Some of the owners started to push forward, but Len stopped them, addressing himself to Nicole.

"How many horses are there?"

"Seven." People began to argue, and Len saw the back door to the house open with Cliff running toward him.

Everything stopped when Len yelled, "Enough!" Then he said, "I have enough room for everyone, so just be patient."

Cliff walked right up to him, speaking softly to Len. "What the hell is all this?"

"Padgett's barn burned down last night, and these people need barn space for their horses." Cliff's eyes widened. "They've got seven horses to board, and there may be more." People were becoming impatient again. "I've got this," Len said. "When they're settled, I'll fill you in." Cliff nodded and walked back to the house just as Geoff was opening the door.

"Okay, before we unload the horses, I have agreements that need to be signed." Len had found them in the tack room after he hung up the phone. "Owners, follow me, and Nicole, the ring's out back if you want to take a look."

She tromped through the barn as Len led the owners to the tack room. He handed each one an agreement, updating the rate by hand, and had them fill it in, sign, and date. Then he collected checks along with the agreements. "Okay, I have five stalls ready, so start unloading, and I'll get the other two set."

Fred had been hanging around. "I need to help Randy."

Love Means ... *Courage*

Len smiled. "I can take it from here. Thanks you for your help." Out front, the first horse was unloaded and walked into the designated stall.

Len began filling the wheelbarrow when one of the young girls who'd arrived with the horses tapped him on the shoulder. "They need you in the barn. I can do that." She grabbed the shovel and began loading the wheelbarrow like a stevedore.

Len went back inside and met Nicole as she walked through the barn. "Nice, clean, and the ring is good." She was actually smiling. "With Padgett, I paid him for the use of the ring and facilities with ten percent of my fees. Is that okay?"

"I think so, sure."

"If you don't mind my asking, why was the barn so empty? It's clean and in good shape. Doesn't make sense to me."

"Remind me and I'll tell you over coffee sometime."

"That's a deal. You bring the story; I'll bring the coffee." They walked to where horses were being unloaded, and Len directed them to stalls. In a surprisingly short time, the barn was filled with horses and their owners, grooming, brushing, and getting their charges settled.

Nicole was looking over the proceedings. "Most of them lost their saddles and tack in the fire, so it could be a while before I'm up to speed again, but we'll get there. You realize you've got additional stall space in back, don't you?" Len shook his head, and she led him to the back half of the barn. One side was definitely set up for feeding cattle. Len figured it was used mostly in the winter. The other side was largely open. "You could easily build an additional four to six stalls in this space if you wanted to expand."

"Good. I'll have to talk to Cliff, and see what he says, but at least we have space to expand." They walked back up the barn where the horses were now settled, and owners were beginning to leave. Len thanked the girls for getting the stalls ready, and after making one more check, walked up to the house.

The door was open, and a pair of eyes peered out through the screen. A small voice piped up with, "Hos."

Cliff appeared behind Geoff and unlatched the door. "He's been bouncing around ever since they arrived." Geoff stepped back, and Len walked into the kitchen. "Can I offer you some coffee?"

"Thanks."

Cliff poured a cup and handed it to Len. "You want to tell me what's going on?"

"Seems Padgett's barn was hit by lightning yesterday, and Nicole called this morning asking if we had space to board five horses, and then seven showed up." He handed Cliff the signed agreements along with the checks. "I collected first and last month's stable fees in advance from all of them, and Nicole will pay you for training privileges in the ring."

Cliff sipped his coffee as Len finished relaying the morning's events. When he was done, he looked over his mug, eyes wandering around the now clean kitchen. "There's something I think you should know," Len said as he put his cup down. "I'm not sure how to handle this, so I'm gonna tell you straight." Cliff put his cup down as well and waited. "When we were at lunch yesterday, we heard a rumor that the farm's in financial trouble." Len picked up his cup again and sipped, needing something to keep his hands busy. "I know it's none of my business, and I thought about whether I should say anything at all."

Cliff exploded, pounding his fist on the table. "Damn busybodies and their gossip!" Len jumped in surprise, and Geoff started to cry. Cliff lifted his son onto his lap, trying to soothe him, even as Len could see the tide of anger rising in Cliff's eyes.

Love Means ... *Courage*

"I've known you a long time, and Ruby was my best friend. The only reason I brought it up was to offer my help. I took accounting and business classes and worked in the Ford dealership business office." He was starting to talk faster, hoping to get his thoughts out before Cliff went off again.

Geoff was still sniffling as Cliff turned him around and got up from his chair. Len followed as Cliff walked through the living room and opened a door to what looked like an office. "I've been trying to get a handle on what my dad was doing for months." The desk was covered with papers and what looked like invoices and bills. "I've paid everything on time, but the money's going out faster than it's coming in."

"Why? There has to be a reason."

"There is." Cliff sat Geoff in a chair and ruffled through a pile of papers. "Dad took out a loan for two hundred fifty thousand dollars right before he died, and I can't find the money. The interest payments are killing us. I've been making the monthly payments, but they're sapping the cash reserves and my savings."

"Did you visit the bank?"

"Yeah, but they don't know what he did with the money. And he used the entire farm as collateral."

Len was starting to see the picture and some of the reasons for Cliff's behavior. "So, if you don't pay...."

Cliff swallowed. "They take the farm."

"The money must be somewhere, or else he bought something with it."

"I know." Cliff was getting testy again. "But I can't find anything." Frustration was clear in his voice.

"Okay. Your father died about a year ago, and his will was probated. Wouldn't they have to know everything he owned?"

Cliff shook his head. "Dad had the farm put in both our names years ago, so it just reverted to me at his death. What money dad had went to my sisters, and I got the farm."

"And since the debt is secured by the farm, you inherited that too."

Cliff nodded, looking miserable. "I lost my wife, father, and inherited this mess all at the same time."

Before Len could think—and his need for self-preservation could stop him—he stepped to Cliff and pulled the man into a hug. He didn't know what else he could do, but the man was hurting and needed some reassurance. To his surprise, Cliff hugged him back, and Len felt his traitorous body react immediately.

"It's okay, Cliff." When he realized what he'd done, Len stepped away and looked at the floor, totally at a loss, mumbling, "We'll figure something out." He had to figure out how he could leave the room to hide his embarrassment. Cliff had to have felt him; how could he not have?

Len looked up from the floor, watching Cliff as he walked behind the desk. "I just don't know where to start anymore. For the life of me, I can't find what he could have spent the money on." Cliff picked up some more papers. "Of course, there's also the normal operating loans that are due at the end of the season, but with these interest payments on the mortgage, the money I was trying to set aside's been going for them. Every month I'm going further in the hole."

Len breathed a sigh of relief that Cliff was too distracted to notice. Despite what had happened years earlier and what Len desperately wanted to happen, he knew that Cliff would never return his feelings. Cliff had been married, had a child, and would probably marry again.

He tried to get his thoughts in order and away from his now rampant libido. "If you were your dad and took out a loan for that kind of money, what would you do with it?"

"Probably use it to enlarge the farm." Cliff went to a file cabinet. "I checked all the deeds, both the copies in the files and the originals in the safe deposit box, and there's nothing new."

"Okay." Len thought for a while. "You have a couple issues here, and I think we need to break them up and handle them one at a time. First, we need to increase the income that the farm brings in so we can meet more of the monthly expenses and increase your cash flow. We got a boost today, and we have room for another horse now. And Nicole told me that we could add six more stalls to the southwest corner of the barn. That'll bring in more income with only a small amount of additional expense, since you're already paying me anyway. We could also bring in some extra one-time cash by selling the excess hay in the loft. Even with the additional horses, we have a year's worth of hay, and we'll start bringing in more in two months."

"Good idea." Cliff was starting to look a little less desperate. "I could put an ad in the paper?"

"No need. There are already plenty of ads for people who need hay. I already checked. All we have to do is answer them."

"Jesus, you've already thought about this, haven't you?"

"I was going to suggest it to you anyway." Len got his mind on his next idea before he lost it. "The next thing we need to do is inventory everything: land, along with its use, equipment, supplies, animals, everything. We need to make sure that we're using everything to the farm's best advantage." He saw the skeptical look on Cliff's face and decided he should go for broke. "You've been in your own world since Ruby and your dad died. Fred and Randy have done their very best for you, but they can only handle what they know about, and I doubt you know all they've been doing. So you need to find out."

"Okay." Cliff lowered himself in the chair, and Geoff climbed on his lap.

"And I think you need to visit the bank again. Money leaves a trail, and we need to follow it."

"They weren't helpful the last time."

That defeatist tone was starting to creep in again, and Len hated it. For a while, he could see some fire behind Cliff's eyes, but now it was like someone had doused them with water. "I'll go with you, if you like." He wasn't sure Cliff would accept his offer, but he made it anyway. Len felt fired up and excited, and he hoped he was inspiring Cliff to action, but he wasn't sure.

"What do we do first?"

Len got up and went into the living room, returning with the Sunday paper Cliff hadn't yet thrown away. "You start making phone calls, turning some of that hay in the loft into cash by answering some ads. If they want it delivered, charge them. It looks like the going rate is almost two dollars a bale."

"How many bales should I sell?"

Len shrugged. "I'm going to go out and take a rough count and figure what we'll need for the next three or four months. We can sell the rest."

"I'll meet you in the barn after I make the calls."

Len got up and left the house, hurrying to the barn. Most of the owners had left, but he found Nicole in one of the stalls, grooming a horse. "Nicole, I was wondering if I could use some of your expertise."

She looked up from what she was doing. "I'm almost done here." The brush flowed easily over the horse's coat. "There you go, Buster, all set." She gave the horse a pat and then left the stall. "How can I help?"

"We've got a lot more hay than we need, and I was wondering if you could help me estimate our needs so we can sell the rest." She nodded and Len led her to the hay loft. At the top of the stairs, Nicole whistled as she looked up at the walls of hay.

"This loft holds about two thousand bales of hay, and it looks like you've got about fifteen hundred still. I'd estimate you could easily sell a thousand bales with no problem." She turned to Len. "Will this be part of that story you promised?"

"Most definitely." They descended the stairs, and Len left Nicole with the horses and walked back to the house, finding Cliff on the phone in the office, just finishing a call.

"I hope I didn't overdo it, but after two calls, I've sold five hundred bales. It seems the long winter left a lot of people short on hay."

"Good. Nicole estimated we could sell a thousand bales with no problem." Len's mind boggled as he thought of the hauling and carrying involved with moving that much hay.

"I quoted then two dollars a bale, two fifty if we had to load it. They're bringing their own people. You'll just need to keep count."

"When will they be here?"

"One's coming today at two and another tomorrow at three. We can reassess then."

Len spent the rest of the day helping get the hay out of the loft and recording the major items for their inventory. He didn't see Cliff or Geoff, and he hoped Cliff was out looking at the fields. At four, the last of the hay they'd sold was loaded, and Len had a check in his pocket. The hay wagon pulled away, and Len saw Cliff pull into the driveway and get out of the truck with Geoff right behind him. "That made a dent in the hay loft." He handed Cliff the check as Geoff ran into the barn, looking at the horses.

"I bet it did. I visited all the fields and did find some that we can put to work. It's about fifty acres, but it'll help." Cliff gripped his shoulder, smiling at him, and Len was gripped by that same fluttery feeling in his stomach as the heat from Cliff's hand seeped through his shirt. "Thank you, Len."

"For what?"

"Waking me up and getting me off my useless ass." Len felt Cliff's fingers rubbing against his shoulder. The movement may have been innocent, but to Len it felt incredibly erotic. He knew he should pull away and get the last of the day's work done, but he didn't want to do anything to break the contact. The crunch of tires pulled Len from his thoughts, and Cliff lowered his hand.

"Janelle," Cliff called, and Len turned, watching as she got out of the car.

"Hi, Cliff." She gave her brother a hug. "Hi, Len." He smiled and waved. "You haven't called, so I stopped by to see how you were doing." She walked to Len, smiling brightly.

Cliff interrupted and grinned at him. "He's been busy kicking my ass for three days."

"I'm sorry. I should have called and thanked you. Let me make it up to and take you to dinner on Friday."

"I'd like that."

Love Means ... *Courage*

"Aun' Nell." Geoff raced out of the barn and threw himself around her legs. She looked slightly panicked and tentatively stroked his head. He lifted himself away and took her hand, pulling her toward the barn. "Hos."

She let Geoff show her the horses before heading back to her car, looking at Len. "I'll see you Friday." She smiled at him and then climbed in her car and drove away.

"She likes you." Len hadn't heard Cliff approach, and he jumped slightly.

Shit, that was the last thing he needed. "We're just friends."

"I don't think she sees it that way." God, just what he didn't want—Janelle getting ideas that he was interested in her. But as he watched her car pull out of the driveway, he began looking at her behavior in a different light, and what he saw scared him.

Geoff tugged on his pant leg. "Wen hossie wide."

Len bent down and picked up the toddler, bouncing him in the air. "Yup." Len looked at Cliff and found him smiling. "Let's go saddle Misty, and I'll give you a horsie ride."

"Yay!"

For the time being, other concerns faded away in the glow of little Geoff's happiness.

CHAPTER 7

"I DON'T know what to do, Mom." Len sat on the sofa in their living room, holding his head in his hands. "I'm so damned confused." He'd been floundering for the last week and even more so since his dinner with Janelle on Friday.

She sat down next to him, her hand on his back, "I know you are, honey, but that comes with the territory. When you told me you were gay, I already knew. But the confirmation was still a bit of a shock, even though I tried to keep it from you."

"Why didn't you tell me?" He worried that he might have hurt her.

She took his hand, squeezing it gently in hers. "Because it was more important at the time for you to know that it didn't really matter to me, that I'd love you no matter what, and with time I understood. The thing is: you being honest with me meant you no longer had to hide, at least with me."

"That doesn't really help me." His head was starting to pound.

Love Means ... *Courage*

"Doesn't it?" Len lifted his head as his mother spoke. "You need to be honest with yourself and those in your life. Remember how happy you were once Ruby knew and you could talk about things with her, and just be yourself without the hiding and the lying?"

He sighed loudly. "Yeah, I do." God, he missed her.

"Most people would tell you to be quiet and keep it to yourself, and to a degree that's true. You don't have to flaunt that you're gay, but you don't have to hide either. You need to decide how you want to live your life: scared and alone or open and honest." She patted his knee and got up from the sofa. "Only you can decide what's right for you, not me or anyone else." She turned off the television. "I'm going to bed. I'll see you tomorrow." She patted his shoulder gently, and then he heard her steps as she walked to her bedroom and closed the door.

Len sat quietly without moving, thinking things over. He liked his job at the farm and didn't want to lose it. It was hard work, but he was learning so much from Nicole, and he and the guys were becoming a team. They'd sold off most of the extra hay, and together he and Cliff had decided to hold off on the rest, particularly since they used some of the money to build the extra stalls in the barn.

Word was already getting around, and they'd added another horse just yesterday, bringing the total to twelve, with four new horse stalls and two pony stalls almost ready. And tomorrow Cliff had an appointment at the bank, and he had asked Len to go along.

The hardest thing was the way he was beginning to feel about Cliff. They'd worked together to build the new stalls, relocating Geoff's sandbox nearby to keep him occupied.

"Damn it, Len, practice what you preach. You gave Cliff grief for hiding and living in his own world, while you're doing the exact same thing." With a small grunt, he lifted his work weary-muscles off the sofa and headed to bed. There was a lot to get done in the morning before their appointment at the bank.

LEN woke at his usual time and quietly got ready for work, eating something, packing his lunch, and throwing an extra set of clothes in his car before driving to the farm. As usual, it was still dark when he arrived, but the horses were already active, and he turned them out in the pastures and began the constant job of mucking out stalls. He cleaned out the worst of the stalls and spot-cleaned the others before filling water troughs and feeding the few horses that stayed inside. At seven, he heard the barn door open, and the guys joined him for what had become their regular morning planning session. Len had told Cliff about these, but as yet, he hadn't attended one. Len always gave him a recap when he saw him later in the day, though.

"Before I forget, will one of you be able to stay close later this morning? I need to go into town with Cliff for a while."

Randy looked curious, but it was Fred who actually asked the question. "Does this have anything to do with the rumors going around town?"

"Yes. We don't know much right now, but I'm trying to help figure out what's going on." The guys nodded and seemed content with the answer, but Len continued. "I'll ask Cliff to talk to you once he knows something."

"Thanks, Len." The guys got to work, and Len went back to the stalls.

He liked to get the heavy work done early in the day when it was cooler. He was almost done when he heard a familiar voice, "Wen!" followed by the patter of small steps. He stood up, and small arms wrapped around a leg. "Wen!"

Love Means ... *Courage*

"Hi, Geoff." He picked up the toddler and gave him a carrot to feed one of the horses as Cliff approached from behind him. A familiar electric tingle went up his spine before lodging in his stomach, fading into the now familiar butterflies. "Morning, Cliff." He didn't turn around and watched as Geoff fed the horse his treat.

"We should leave for the bank soon." Len thought he heard a tinge of worry in his voice, which was fully understandable under the circumstances. "I don't know what they're going to tell us this time that they couldn't the last time."

Len shrugged and set Geoff back down. "Sometimes it's the questions you ask." He turned to face Cliff. "As I told you before, money has a trail. We need to try to follow it, and the trail starts at the bank." Len began walking to put his tools away, and Cliff followed. "I don't know what we'll find, but I promised you I'd help."

"Geoff, come back here. We'll be leaving in a few minutes." Those little legs stopped in their tracks and he ran back to Cliff.

"Twuck?"

"Yes, we're going in the truck." Cliff picked up his son before continuing, turning to Len. "I've been wondering why you're helping me. I don't mean to sound ungrateful, because I appreciate it, but…." He stammered before continuing. "I mean, in the short time you've been here, you've already done so much."

Len put the tools in their places and turned around to face Cliff, noticing for the first time a look he didn't quite understand. A million answers to Cliff's question flashed through his mind, but he took what he thought was the safest. "Ruby was my best friend, and she loved both you and this farm very much."

"Oh."

God, he wanted to tell Cliff what he truly felt and see if his lips felt like they did for that brief moment in high school, but he couldn't, and he felt like a coward. "I should change before we go." Len walked toward his car. "I'll meet you at your truck in ten minutes."

"Okay. I'll get Geoff ready to go and meet you at the truck." Cliff turned and walked back toward the house while Len headed into the tack room. Once inside, he pulled off his work pants and shirt before changing into a pair of pants and shirt he'd worn when he worked at the dealership. It had only been a few weeks, but it seemed like a lifetime since he'd worked there.

As he finished getting ready, Len smiled to himself. He liked it here on the farm, working outside in the fresh air, and he felt like he was making a difference or at least helping. He never felt that way before.

After running his fingers through his hair nervously, he folded his clothes, leaving them on the chair, and walked through the barn, meeting Nicole on his way. They exchanged greetings, and he told her he'd be gone for a few hours. She met his smile and told him not to worry; she'd watch things while he was gone.

Cliff was strapping Geoff into his seat as Len approached the truck, and a few minutes later, they were all on their way into town with Geoff in his car seat between them, talking a blue streak the entire time as he pointed out every horse or cow they passed.

In town, Cliff drove directly to the bank and parked the truck, getting Geoff out of his seat before leading the way into the bank and approaching one of the tellers. "Can I help you?" The middle-aged woman smiled her "customer" smile.

"I, er, we have an appointment with Gordon Frisk."

"Ah, I see." She closed her window and came out through a small swinging door before leading them into a small office. "Please have a seat; he'll be with you in a few minutes." Cliff thanked her and then sat down with Geoff held tightly on his lap like a shield.

"Morning, Cliff, what can I do for you?" A man in his late thirties entered the office, speaking cheerfully as he shook hands and sat behind his desk.

"My father took a large mortgage against the farm just before he died, and we can't find any trace of the money, or what he did with it. I was hoping you could help us?"

The man opened a file on his desk. "As I told you when you were in before...." Len nearly bristled at his tone but kept to himself. "Your father took out the mortgage against the farm but wouldn't tell us what he planned to use the money for. I think it was something he wanted to keep quiet."

Because everyone in this town, including your employees, have big mouths, Len thought, but again he kept quiet.

Cliff looked to Len, who took that as a signal to go ahead. "When you paid out the money, did he put it in one of his accounts, or did he take it as a check?"

Gordon checked through his file and then consulted the huge computer on his desk. "It appears he had it deposited into a savings account."

Len spoke up. "Can you get the statements for that account? It would help to see when and how the money was withdrawn." *You'd think a banker could figure things like this out for himself and be remotely helpful.*

"Give me a minute to look through the files." Gordon got up and left the office.

Len turned to Cliff. "Don't you have copies of the bank statements?"

"Some, but not all of them. Dad tended to do things his own way, and he kept a lot of things in his head." Geoff began to squirm, and Cliff pulled a truck out of his pocket and let Geoff play on the floor near his chair. "If dad would have kept better records, I wouldn't be in this mess."

"You need to set up a filing system to organize everything. Maybe hire an accountant to help you set something up that you could maintain yourself."

Their conversation was cut off when Gordon came back in the office carrying a bundle of papers. "Here are copies of the statements." He sat at his desk and began to go through them. "Here's where he deposited the money." He looked further, shifting to a different statement. "And it looks like he withdrew all but a thousand dollars a month later." He handed over the statement for Cliff to see, and Cliff passed it to Len.

"How did he make the withdrawal?" Len asked. Gordon shrugged, and Len rolled his eyes, not hiding his annoyance from the banker. "Did he take it as cash and stuff it in a briefcase?"

"Not likely."

"Well, then he must have either purchased a cashier's check or a money order. You should have a record of those, and we need a copy." Len handed back the statement copy.

The light finally seemed to go on and Gordon smiled for the first time. "Ah, yes. I'll be right back." Geoff was still playing, crawling around on the floor, making engine noises. Cliff appeared nervous and didn't seem in the mood to talk, so Len sat and waited.

"I found it." Gordon again sat behind his desk. "It was made out to Mason County Title." He handed the copy directly to Len this time.

Love Means ... *Courage*

Len stood up. "Can we keep this?" Len handed the copy to Cliff, who glanced at it, turned white, then handed it back.

"Yes. I made that copy for you." He stood as well and shook Len's hand. Cliff stood up, moving in a daze as he, too, shook the manager's hand, and then he gathered Geoff's things before taking his hand and walking out of the bank without saying a word.

"Thank you for your help," Len told Gordon before he turned and followed Cliff out of the bank.

"Well, that was useless." Cliff leaned against the truck, looking drained.

"No, Cliff, this tells us a lot. It tells us that your father purchased land and that Mason County Title handled the transaction. All we need to do is contact them to see what he bought." Cliff wasn't listening. "What is it?"

Cliff lifted Geoff into his seat and strapped him in before climbing into the truck, saying nothing. Len didn't press and got in as well, closing the door with a thunk.

"The date on the check is the day before he died."

"Holy cow—you don't think...?"

Cliff sighed and turned the key in the ignition, "Let's find out." He pulled out of the parking lot and drove the block down the street, pulling into Mason County Title and turning off the engine.

"Daddy?" Geoff seemed to sense his father's uneasiness and handed him the toy truck he'd been carrying. "Feew bedder?"

Cliff took the toy and smiled back at his son. "Thank you." Cliff then kissed Geoff on the cheek and unhooked him from the seat. After thunking the truck doors closed, they walked across to the entrance.

Inside the small-house-turned-into-an-office, there didn't appear to be anyone around. Len coughed lightly and waited until an attractive young woman walked in from another of the rooms. "Can I help you?"

Geoff was squirming to get down, so Len did the talking. "We need a copy of the documentation for a real estate closing. It would have been done in this office a little over a year ago." Len handed her the copy of the cashier's check. "The purchaser would be Carter Laughton."

"Oh my goodness, yes." Her eyes lit as she turned to Cliff. "You're Carter's son, Cliff. I'm Jeanie Hudson. I used to babysit for you when you were his age." She tickled Geoff gently, and he squirmed and giggled. "I'm sorry about your dad."

"Thanks. It seems like he purchased some real estate, but I don't have a record of the purchase."

She walked to a nearby file cabinet and pulled open a drawer. "I should have it right here. Yes." She pulled out a file folder and opened it. "It'll take me a few minutes to make copies and get them certified, and I'll have to charge you."

"It's okay. I just need the copies. Umm, can you tell me the date of the closing?"

She consulted the file. "March twenty-fourth of last year." She left and went to make copies.

"I know why I don't have copies of anything." Len turned and looked into Cliff's face, waiting for him to continue. "That's the day dad died. I bet he and Ruby were on their way home from the closing when they got into the accident."

"Why didn't they get the papers from the car?"

"There wasn't much left of it, or the tree, and I doubt anyone bothered to look."

Love Means ... *Courage*

Len turned away and quietly shifted in his chair. *What on earth could you say to that? "I'm sorry" doesn't begin to cover it.* So he sat quietly and waited until the clerk came back out and handed him the copies.

"I notarized the deed, so it's official. The purchase was registered a year ago." She looked over the paperwork. "The taxes for last year were paid at closing, but there will be property taxes due in the next couple months. Looks like you caught it just in time." Cliff took out his wallet, but she stilled his hand. "Don't worry about it." They thanked her again, leaving the office and climbing back in the truck. At least the mystery of the missing money was solved.

"Why was Ruby with him at the closing?" Len asked.

Cliff unlocked the truck and opened his door. "I don't think we'll ever know, but there is a question we can answer. What did he buy?" Len fastened his seat belt and waited while Cliff looked through the papers and let out a whistle. "He bought the Henderson farm. Holy sh—" Cliff stopped himself from swearing just in time. "He bought all the land and buildings, 320 acres, for a quarter million dollars, and it includes the house." Cliff put down the papers and started the engine, pulling out of the parking lot and heading back to the farm.

"Why don't you drop me at the barn, and then you can go take a look," Len suggested. Cliff remained quiet as he drove, and Len sank into his own thoughts.

They pulled into the farm a few minutes later and Len got out of the truck, closing the door. Cliff leaned over and opened the window. "Thank you, Len."

"No problem." He smiled back at Cliff. "I'm glad I could help." The window raised, and Geoff waved good-bye. Len returned the wave before going into the barn, changing his clothes and eating his lunch before returning to work.

THE day was winding down, and Len was exhausted as he put away the tools and brought in the horses for the night, settling them in their stalls with fresh water and hay. He was just bringing in the last animal when he heard a vehicle pull into the driveway. He glanced down the aisle and thought he saw Cliff's truck but wasn't sure. Finishing up, he made sure all the stall doors were closed and latched before closing up the barn and walking to his car.

"Len." Cliff walked across the yard. As he turned, he noticed other cars pull into the driveway. "Would you come inside and join us for a drink?"

Len recognized Janelle's car. He had been trying to avoid her but agreed against his better judgment. "Thanks. That would be nice." He followed Cliff inside the house, now alive with conversation and people.

Janelle saw him and rushed over, taking him by the arm and introducing him to her sisters, Victoria and Mari, along with Victoria's husband, Dan. Victoria was pregnant, and Dan hovered over her.

"I was wondering when you'd call me," Janelle flirted when she'd completed the introductions.

"I've been very busy and really tired. I'm sorry." Unlike the last time, he didn't set a day and time for dinner. He did not want to give her the wrong idea.

Cliff came to his rescue. "Len, would you like a beer?"

"That would be nice, thanks." Cliff handed him a beer, and he took a seat on the sofa, purposely sitting away from Janelle.

Love Means ... *Courage*

Cliff spoke to everyone. "I called you because I wanted you to know that today, with Len's help, we figured out what happened to the money dad borrowed on the farm. He used it to buy the Henderson place."

Janelle leaned forward in her chair, "So that means that we each own a quarter of the Henderson farm. We should resell it and get the money back."

Cliff sat down. "No. It means that the farm now includes the Henderson's land and house. Dad used a loan against the farm to pay for the land, so the land becomes part of the farm."

"Then why are you telling us? So you could rub our noses in it?" This was a side of Janelle Len had never seen before, and it wasn't pretty.

"That's enough, Janelle!" Cliff's youngest sister, Mari, piped in, and then she turned to Cliff. "What is it you want to tell us?"

"Just that dad and Ruby were on their way home from the closing when he died."

"So what are you going to do?"

"I don't know. I just wanted to let you know what I found out."

"It's not fair." Janelle continued.

"What isn't?" Mari stood up, glaring at her. "Cliff's been paying on that loan for the last year, and while he has the land, he also has the debt to go along with it. Do you want to work the Henderson farm and pay the debt?"

"No, but—"

"I didn't think so." Mari turned to Len. "I'm sorry you had to see this."

"It's okay. I'm just glad I could help find out what happened."

"We all appreciate it." Mari looked toward the kitchen, "I'm going to start dinner." She looked at Cliff. "I bet he and Geoff haven't had a decent meal in weeks. Please join us."

"Thank you."

"Janelle, why don't you give me a hand?" Len watched as Janelle plastered a smile onto her face and followed Mari into the kitchen.

"Wen!" Small feet raced across the room before Geoff launched himself onto Len's lap. "Hos." He held out the plastic horse for Len to see. "Hos."

"That's a nice horse. It looks like Misty, doesn't it?" Geoff nodded vigorously and hugged Len around the neck before climbing down, racing away into the kitchen.

"Aun' Mawi, Aun' 'Nell. Hos, hos."

Len felt sort of out of place with Cliff's family and didn't know what to do. It looked to Len like Cliff felt the same way as he sat quietly in his chair, looking down at the beer in his hand.

They ate quietly at the kitchen table with Mari, Cliff, and Dan carrying most of the conversation. Len joined in occasionally, with Janelle sitting next to him—either glaring at her brother or talking softly to Len. As the meal progressed, their conversation lightened up, and thankfully, some of the tension dissipated.

After dinner, Janelle asked Len to walk her to her car, and Cliff's other sisters left as well. After saying good night, he closed Janelle's door, and she pulled away.

"She really seems to like you."

Len turned around and looked at Cliff. "We're just friends."

Love Means ... *Courage*

"I think she thinks there's more to it than that." He could hear the slight protective tone in Cliff's voice. "She may be a pain, but she's my sister."

"I know, and I'm not trying to hurt her, but we could never be more than friends. And I've never led her to believe otherwise. We talk and occasionally go out to dinner, but I've never touched her or even kissed her." Len suppressed a shudder.

"Oh. Is there something wrong? Because she really seems to like you."

"Well, kinda, I guess." Len ran his hand along the back of his neck. This was one of those man-or-mouse moments, and Len had to choose. "Cliff, I'm gay."

Len waited to see how Cliff would react. Would he fire him on the spot and kick him off the property? Would he hit him? Would he repeat what he'd done in high school and kiss him? He stared at Cliff, waiting for some sort of reaction.

"Oh, um, ah—I'll see you tomorrow." Cliff turned and walked back into the house, the door closing quietly behind him.

Len blinked and stared at the closed door. Cliff just walking away was the last thing he expected. In a sort of daze, Len turned around and walked to his car, driving home without really remembering anything.

CHAPTER 8

THREE days. Len's alarm woke him, and he automatically got out of bed. Three days—that's how long it had been since he'd told Cliff he was gay. Three days of Cliff avoiding him, staying in the house and not coming out, not even acknowledging him. He could take that, but it was also three days since Cliff had let Geoff outside, at least while he was there. No visits to let him see the horses, nothing. Len was completely at a loss for what to do. Part of him said to just keep his head low and work, but he'd done that before. Hell, he'd done that most of his life.

Putting his feet on the floor, he padded to the bathroom for his morning routine before getting dressed. Opening his bedroom door, he quietly walked to the small kitchen, surprised to see his mother sitting at the table. "What are you doing up so early."

"I wanted to talk to you." She pushed back the chair and Len sat down. "I feel responsible for how you're feeling."

Len poured a mug of coffee from the percolator sitting on the table. "Why?"

"I feel like I pushed you into telling Cliff with my advice."

Love Means ... *Courage*

Len slipped his hand over hers. "No. You were right. I may lose my job and someone I was coming to regard as a friend, but you were right nonetheless." He patted her hand and got up, getting himself something to eat. "I just couldn't live a lie any more." He opened the refrigerator and got out the milk for cereal, and then he got a bowl out of the cupboard and poured a big helping of cornflakes. "I'm not the first to feel this way and I won't be the last. Tim told me once that coming out was good, but it came at a cost, and now I see what he meant." Len poured the milk and began to eat.

"That reminds me." She got up and returned with a small piece of paper. "A Tim called last night and left you a number. He asked you to call him back when you had a chance." She placed it near his hand. "He said he gets up early, and that it would be okay to call him before work." She got up and walked back toward her bedroom, smiling as she turned back, watching Len eat faster.

Once his breakfast was done, he put his dishes in the sink, checked his watch, and picked up the phone. His fingers fumbled as he dialed the number, and he had to start over, but finally the call connected. "Tim, it's Len."

He could almost hear the smile come through the phone. "Of course it is. How are you? How's the car dealership?"

"They laid me off, and I'm working as the stable manager at a farm. I like it." Len tried to keep his confusion out of his voice.

"But...."

"I'm working for Cliff Laughton." He wasn't sure if Tim would remember.

"Isn't that the guy who kissed you behind the barn in high school?"

He did remember. "Yeah." Len let a soft sigh travel along the line. "He got married a few years ago and has a little boy named Geoff, but his wife was killed in an accident about a year ago."

"So he's available."

"I guess, but I'm not sure of anything. Whenever he's nearby, I get these fluttery feelings in my stomach, and whenever we work together, I sometimes think I catch him looking at me." Len wasn't sure of anything right now, particularly not after the last three days.

"Have you told him anything?" Len could hear Tim moving around and figured he was getting dressed for work.

Len began talking faster. "That's the kicker. His sister and I are friends, and Cliff said he thought that she wanted to be more than friends."

"Slow down, Lenny, it's okay."

He took a deep breath. "The long and short of it is that I told Cliff I was… gay." He involuntarily hesitated before saying the last word.

"Good for you. And how did it feel?"

Len thought before answering. "Scary and liberating all at the same time."

"Yeah, that's a good description. How did he react?"

"That's the weird part. He said he'd see me in the morning and then went into the house. That was three days ago, and I haven't seen him since. I think he's avoiding me." The confusion he'd been feeling for the last three days came back with a vengeance. "The other guys have seen him briefly, but I haven't seen him or Geoff at all." He heard Tim's light chuckle drift through the phone. "It's not funny!"

Love Means ... *Courage*

"Okay, I'm sorry. I'll try to explain a few things. First, that tingly feeling is your gaydar. Sort of an innate feeling you get when you're around another gay man."

"But Cliff was married to my best friend."

"That doesn't mean much. Not when society puts such pressure on people to be normal. Anyway, here's my advice: give this Cliff a few more days and see what happens. You're going to have to wait him out. I know it's hard, but be patient and keep yourself busy. The ice will thaw; you just have to give it time."

Len realized he was being rude, monopolizing the conversation with his problems. "Thanks. So how's Chicago? Have you met anyone?"

"Actually, I did. His name's Charlie, and he's a little younger than me. We went out once, and he asked me out again this weekend."

"Sounds really nice."

"He is." Len heard a shuffling noise on Tim's side of the line. "I have to get going, or I'll be late, but it was good talking to you. I'll call soon, and you can tell me what happens with Cliff."

"Okay, thanks for the advice."

"No problem. I'm here if you need me."

Len smiled as he hung up the phone. He checked his watch, grabbed his lunch and put it in his cooler along with drinks, and headed to his car.

The farm was still quiet when he arrived, not that he'd expect anything less. The nights were becoming warmer, and on Nicole's advice, many of the horses were left in the pastures overnight. He did a quick check that they were all okay and used the reprieve to clean the last of the stalls. The barn was now nearly full with sixteen horses and a pony. There was only one pony stall empty.

He was sweeping out the barn when the guys arrived, pulling into the drive. "Morning, Randy, Fred."

"Morning, Len." They both looked around the barn, inhaling deeply. It did smell nice, all clean and fresh. Well, as fresh as a barn can be.

"I'm caught up here. Do you guys need some help?"

Fred spoke up. "God, do we. With the extra fields from the Henderson place, we've got a week to get everything planted, and we were talking yesterday, wondering if you'd be willing to help with the field preparation and planting. The tractor will be going from dawn to dusk unless it rains."

"If you'll show me how to drive it, I'll be glad to help."

Both Fred and Randy smiled with relief as Fred pulled out a sheet of paper. "This is the plan, and we need to get all this done in ten days." Fred took some time to explain things to Len while Randy got the tractor out of the shed, filled the tank, started the engine, and took off on the drive. "He's going to get started, and after lunch, we'll show you what needs to be done and how to operate the tractor." Fred folded up the plan and handed it to Len. "I figured you'd be the best one to keep track of our progress." Fred walked toward his truck. "I'll be out in the south pastures fixing fences if you need me."

Fred waved and climbed into the truck, and as he drove away, Len couldn't help looking toward the house. The windows were open, and he could see movement and hear Geoff making "broom, broom" sounds as he played with his trucks. He took a step toward the back door and stopped himself. He couldn't force Cliff to accept him, and he'd be damned if he'd try. Turning on his heel, he marched back into the barn and started feeding and watering the horses still in their stalls.

LEN spent much of the next two days busy as hell. He worked in the barn in the mornings and spent most of the afternoon in the seat of the tractor, disking and planting. Acre after acre passed under his seat, and he didn't get out until the sun was down. He kept track of every field planted or disked on the sheet of paper Fred had given him. The light was fading fast, and he turned around to check on the planter. Everything appeared fine as he made the final pass around the outside of the field. At the last second he turned off the planter and exited the field as a low rumble sounded in the distance. "Good timing," he said to himself as he hightailed it back toward the farm. The field he'd been planting was one of the farthest from the farmhouse.

The rain was just starting as he pulled the tractor into the shed. With the planter on the back, it was too long to fit, but the guys were already back at the farm, so the four of them covered the planter with a huge tarp and tied it down with bungee cords. Fred and Randy ran for the house while Len walked into the barn and opened the pasture doors, guiding the horses into their stalls and shutting the doors. As he was bringing in the last horse, the sky opened up, and the raindrops beat hard on the barn roof. "It's okay, guys. I've got fresh hay and treats." A few of the horses were restless, but Len's voice seemed to soothe them. He placed hay in all the mangers and gave each horse a carrot, patting noses and talking to them. Once each one was fed, watered, and settled, he made sure all the doors were closed and turned out the lights. Standing in the doorway, he watched the lightning as it lit the eastern sky and the now gentle rain fell.

"Hey, Len."

He looked in the direction of the house and saw Cliff standing in the doorway. Cliff waved Len over, and Len sighed, closed the barn door, and jogged toward the house.

"Come inside before you get soaked." Cliff held the door, and Len jogged up the steps and into the back mudroom, where he took off his wet shoes and hung up his dripping coat.

He couldn't look at Cliff and felt very self-conscious, that is, until he heard little feet running across the floor. "Wen!" Geoff's little body bounded against him, little arms hugging his legs.

"Hi, Geoffy."

Those big eyes looked up at him, and Geoff began talking really fast. Len couldn't make out a single word, but the excitement came through just fine.

"We're in the living room." Cliff walked through the kitchen, and Len picked Geoff up, getting a big hug as he carried him into the other room. "Have a seat, Len." Cliff handed him a mug, and Len sat on the sofa, with Geoff jumping up next to him. "How's the planting coming?" Cliff looked over his mug as he sipped.

Randy and Fred both looked at Len, who put his mug down and took out the paper he'd been using to mark their progress. "The existing fields are planted and ready. The new fields that were part of the Henderson farm have been disked and will be planted as soon as we can get back in the fields. We can probably get done in a day, day-and-a-half." Len felt he needed to be formal, like he was giving a presidential briefing or something.

Cliff whistled softly. "That was fast."

Len was about to answer, but Randy beat him to it. "We taught Len to drive the tractor, and he wouldn't come in until it was too dark to see. Hell, I even caught him eating dinner yesterday sitting on the tractor so he wouldn't have to stop." Len was looking at the floor and didn't see the look of surprised admiration that Cliff flashed his way. "He's kept the barn chores up to date and helped us get the planting done." Geoff pulled Len's gaze from the floor when he began to run one of his trucks along Len's arm, and he turned and began running the truck along Geoff's stomach as giggles and squeals of delight filled the room.

Fred and Randy stood up, drawing Len's attention away from Geoff. "We're going to head out." Fred elbowed Randy in the side. "The big guy here has a date with Shell tonight." Randy smiled and clammed up, but he was obviously quite happy. They both left, putting their mugs in the sink on their way out.

Len got up to leave as well; he just didn't feel very comfortable right now. But at least Cliff seemed to be talking to him again, or was that just because Fred and Randy were around? Geoff scooted off the couch and ran into the kitchen, jumping up and down near the table.

Cliff stood up and walked into the kitchen. "I need to make Geoff's dinner." Len followed and put his mug in the sink, getting ready to go. "Would you stay for dinner? I need to get him fed, and then we can talk once he's in bed." Len nodded and looked at Cliff's face. He knew that look; he'd seen it a few weeks before. Well, at least he'd get a last meal this time. "Would you take Geoff in the living room while I get things ready? It shouldn't take too long."

Len repressed a sigh and took Geoff's hand, the youngster pulling him toward his toys. Geoff plopped himself on the floor and began running his trucks around the carpet. After a few minutes, he looked up at Len as if to say, "Why aren't you playing?" With a smile, Len sat on the floor and played cars with Geoff until he heard Cliff call that dinner was ready. Geoff didn't look up, so Len picked him up and flew him into the kitchen, accompanied by peals of laughter and giggles. Len lowered him toward the high chair.

"No baby, big boy."

Len looked to Cliff, who smiled. "He wants a regular chair instead of the high chair." Cliff walked over and spoke directly to Geoff. "You need to use the high chair until you can eat without making a mess."

Len watched as that little head bowed resignedly, and Geoff then climbed in the chair and let Cliff put on the tray. Cliff put a sippy cup and a bowl of macaroni and cheese in front of Geoff, who immediately began to eat, but Len noticed he was careful not to spill. *He must really want to use a big boy chair.* Len looked to Cliff, impressed.

"He really hates the high chair, but he forgets what he's doing when he uses a regular chair." Cliff put a plate in front of Len and then placed his own on the table.

Len began eating, his appetite returning full force as soon as the first bite hit his stomach. "Did you make this?" Len pointed to the roasted pork chops.

"No. Mari did. She helps out when she can."

Len poured coffee, and they ate quietly. Len was still wondering what Cliff wanted to talk about, and while he wasn't so sure he was going to be fired, he still couldn't quite figure it out.

Cliff's voice pulled him out of his whirling curiosity and anxiety. "I've been thinking that I'd like to increase the size of the cattle herd to make use of the new pasture land. We could easily add a hundred and fifty head with no problem, but we need additional grain storage to get us through the winter."

"Why? You've got enough here to support the existing herd, right?" Cliff nodded as he ate. "Doesn't the Henderson place have silos? You could use those—after all, you own them." Len cut a piece of the pork chop.

Love Means ... *Courage*

"I know, but they won't be close to where we need the feed. They're at the far edge of the herd."

Len swallowed. "But you could use them until you get the money together to have them moved here. They looked new to me."

"They were; he just built them a few years ago." Cliff continued eating while he thought. "That's not a bad idea. Now that I know what dad did with the money he borrowed and the additional acreage should provide more than enough money to pay off the loan, I should be able to afford to do that in a year or so." Geoff cut off their conversation as he banged on this tray, giggling when they both looked at him.

"You just wanted attention, didn't you?" Cliff leaned to his son and blew a raspberry on his cheek. "You need to finish eating." Geoff turned and blew a sticky raspberry on Cliff's cheek before returning to his food. Cliff laughed deeply and wiped his face as he returned to his dinner.

The rest of the meal was fairly quiet with Geoff garnering most of the attention. When Geoff was finished, Cliff wiped the boy's face and let him out of the chair. He ran into the living room, and soon the "broom, broom" and brake screech noises filtered into the kitchen.

Len and Cliff finished eating, and Cliff put the dishes in the sink. "I need to get him ready for bed. I'll be right back down." Len watched as Cliff scooped Geoff into his arms and zoomed him up the stairs.

Alone in the living room, Len wandered around looking at the pictures on the walls and sort of pacing off his energy. While he was fairly sure Cliff wasn't going to fire him, he wasn't too sure what he wanted to talk about. He stopped in front of a picture hanging on the wall of Cliff and Ruby, standing with Cliff's father who was holding Geoff. *Maybe he's going to tell me he wants me to stay away from*

Geoff. He heard footsteps on the stairs and turned away from the photograph. "Is he okay?"

"Out like a light." Cliff stepped off the last stair and walked to Len.

"I...." The both began talking at the same time, and Cliff put up his hand. "Len, I'm sorry." It sounded to him like Cliff was going to continue. Maybe he *was* going to fire him. "I'm sorry, I turned my back to you the other day, and I'm sorry for avoiding you this week."

This was not at all what Len had expected, and he had to check to make sure his mouth wasn't hanging open like a fish. "It's okay," he stammered, trying to process Cliff's meaning.

"No, it's not. What you did showed courage. Telling me you were gay took guts. Guts I wish I'd had, so I owe you an apology. I'm sorry for turning my back on you. I'm sorry for avoiding you, and most of all, I'm sorry you had to wait five years."

"For what?"

Cliff didn't answer him. Instead, he leaned forward and kissed him. His lips were tentative at first, like Cliff wasn't sure his advance would be welcomed, but as the kiss continued, Len moaned very softly and answered the kiss with his own. Then he felt Cliff's arms around him, a hand sliding through his hair as the kiss deepened, and Cliff pressed his whole body against Len's, touching from toes to tummy to lips. Len could barely believe he was actually getting what he'd wanted ever since that night behind the barn. Cliff Laughton was kissing him. Hell, not just kissing him—it felt like he was trying to short-circuit his brain. All too quickly, he felt the pressure on his lips ease, and Cliff stepped back, looking into his eyes.

Len was breathing hard, his thoughts whirling, his eyes locked on Cliff's. "Don't make me wait another five years, okay?"

Love Means ... *Courage*

Cliff muttered, "I don't intend to," and then kissed him again. This time the kiss was longer and sent a tingling through Len's body. His senses filled with Cliff's scent as he inhaled deeply, his taste as their tongues dueled, the feel of his firm, solid body. Len's head began to swirl with the aroma of sweat, hay, and man as he was guided across the floor and lowered onto the sofa. The assault on his senses increased as he felt Cliff's weight on him, solid and good. Fucking hell, he was making out with Cliff on his sofa. It was everything his young, feverish brain could ever have wished for.

"Daddy."

Len had to give Cliff credit—he didn't jerk away from Len and pretend nothing was happening. Instead he raised his head and peered over the back of the sofa before giving Len another quick kiss and then boosting himself up and onto his feet. "I'll be right there." Before going to Geoff, he extended his hand and helped Len to his feet.

"You need to see to Geoff. I'll let myself out and see you in the morning."

"Daddy." They could only see Geoff's legs and feet on the top stair.

Cliff nodded and gave Len one final kiss. "Thank you." Then he walked up the stairs to where Geoff was standing. Len watched as Cliff climbed the stairs, waiting for him to disappear from sight before walking to the mud room to get his things.

Rain dripped from his hair and dribbled down his back as he settled in the car and shut the door. Len could hardly believe what had just happened. Cliff had kissed him—and not just some soft peck; he'd ravished him. Len could still feel Cliff's heat and taste the salty sweetness of his skin on his tongue. "Wow." Breaking out of his daydreams, he pulled out his keys and started the car, pulling out of the drive and pointing the car toward home.

CHAPTER 9

"HI, MOM." Len closed the door, blocking out the sound of the rain.

She looked away from the television to smile at him. "How was work?" She didn't look worried, but Len noticed that she checked the clock. "You're home late."

"Cliff invited me for dinner." Len slipped off his jacket and hung it to dry.

"So I take it the two of you talked."

Len smiled sheepishly. "You could say that, yeah." He really didn't want to get into details with his mother.

"So things are okay between you?" When Len didn't answer, she turned around in her chair. Len watched as she looked him over and then smiled before turning back to the television without another word.

"I'll see you in the morning." Len went to his room, closing out everything else as the door clicked shut. Len sat on the edge of the bed, pulling off his shoes before leaning back on the mattress and closing his eyes.

Cliff was there again. He could feel his weight on his body, Cliff's lips pulling gently, Cliff's excitement against his hip. "Damn...." Len's pants had gotten tight, painfully tight. Without thinking, Len popped the catch on his jeans and the painful pressure gave way to relief. Sliding his hand down his stomach, he slid his fingers along his length and exposed his arousal to the air. His mind played the scene in Cliff's living room, embellishing it, enhancing it. This time there was no Geoff, just him and Cliff. Their clothes disappeared by magic, and he could feel Cliff's body, stroke his hardness, slide his hands along the curve of his back and over his firm butt. He'd done this so many times before, but now it was so much richer, so real. "Cliff...." Len moaned softly as his climax overpowered him.

Breathing heavily, he collapsed back on the bed, his chest heaving. Pulling his shirt over his head, he wiped himself and basked in the glow of his fantasy before sitting up and undressing the rest of the way. Putting on his robe, he padded to the bathroom and started the shower.

The heated water felt good on his aching muscles as his hands scrubbed his tingling skin. He couldn't stop himself from wondering what Cliff's hands would feel like against his skin. "Len," He heard his mother's voice through the door. "Janelle's on the phone."

Len's fantasy popped like a soap bubble. "I'll be right out." Rinsing himself quickly, he shut off the water and wrapped a towel around his waist before opening the bathroom door and padding to the phone. "Hi, Janelle."

"Hi, Len. I hope I didn't wake you."

"No, I was just cleaning up." He heard the other side of the line go quiet, and he shivered slightly even though the room was warm.

"I was wondering if you'd like to go to the play at the high school on Friday. They're doing *Camelot*, and I thought it might be fun. The show starts at eight." Her voice had definitely deepened.

He hesitated initially. "Sure. I have to work until late, so I'll meet you there." He was dripping all over the floor. "I need to go, but I'll see you Friday at about seven-forty-five."

"Okay, see you then." She hung up the phone, and Len padded back to the bathroom. After drying himself off, he finished his evening routine and went to his bedroom, climbing into bed. He was asleep almost as soon as his head hit the pillow.

THE alarm went off at the usual time, but this morning, Len felt incredibly energized. He'd slept well and had wonderful dreams; ones he hoped would come true soon. Pulling back the curtains, he peered out the window and saw that the sun was just about to peek over the cloudless horizon. Letting the curtain fall, he turned and got dressed.

Twenty minutes, cleaned up, lunch packed, and a cup of coffee later, he was on his way to the farm, singing along with Culture Club on the radio. Pulling into the drive, he parked and headed right to the barn. The entire place was very unsettled. Horses were shifting and stomping around their stalls, and one of them was kicking the stall door. "That's enough, Haven. Calm down." Len approached him, talking the entire time, trying to calm him. The horse stopped kicking, and Len peered into the stall, seeing one of the barn cats lying lifeless against the far wall. At least that explained the nervousness in the barn. "Shhh, it's okay, boy. We'll get you outside." Len expertly slipped on Haven's halter and slowly went to the back of the stall and opened the door. Carefully, he led the nervous horse toward the pasture door and outside.

Love Means ... *Courage*

"What's all the excitement?"

"Hey, Nicole." He peered out of the stall. "Take a look for yourself."

She peered in the stall and tsked. "Poor thing. Must have gotten kicked."

"Yeah, no wonder they're upset." Len got a shovel and picked up the dead cat along with any of the bloodstained bedding and carried it outside. He dug a hole in an out-of-the-way place and buried everything before returning. The barn had definitely quieted now that the scent of blood was no longer in the air.

Nicole had already started to put some of the horses outside. "I have a group lesson in a couple of hours, so these can stay inside." She indicated four of the horses. Len nodded and finished letting the other horses out.

The other guys arrived, and they met out front in the sunshine with Fred wandering around the side of the barn and then returning. "We should be able to get in the fields this afternoon. The ground seems pretty firm yet. Just need to give it a few hours to dry off." Before they could continue, the back door of the house opened; Len saw Cliff step out and help Geoff down the steps.

Geoff took off at a run as soon as his feet hit the ground, arms and legs going as fast as they could. "Wen!" When he got close, he launched himself into Len's arms, laughing to beat the band.

"Hey, Geoffy." Fred raised his hand and Geoff gave him five, followed by Randy.

The smiles lasted until Cliff joined the group. "Randy, get the tractor started and those last fields planted. Fred, check on the cattle. Len," Cliff paused as he looked around, "I'm sure there are stalls to clean."

Well, what the fuck? "Cliff, Fred was just saying that we should wait until this afternoon to make sure the fields are dry enough. Don't need the tractor getting stuck." The glare he got was unmistakable, but Len ignored it and continued. "Randy and Fred have plenty to do until then, and I have stalls to clean and work to do on the ring before Nicole's class." Len tried to keep his voice level and nonconfrontational, particularly since he was still holding Geoff.

Cliff glared at Len, and Len returned it. "What have you got planned for today, Boss?" Fred asked, trying to break the tension, and Len turned his gaze to him, breaking the visual stalemate.

"I'm gonna try and figure out how to keep paying the bills." The "your salaries" part of those bills was definitely implied but not said. Fred coughed and turned away, and both he and Randy headed off to work.

Len put Geoff down, and Cliff took his hand and led him back toward the house with the little guy peering over his shoulder, a look of confusion on his little face. When everyone was gone, Len took a deep breath and let it out before going to work.

Over the next few hours, he raked the riding ring to level the surface and cleaned a few stalls, being sure to sanitize the one with the dead cat. Nicole stopped by as he was finishing up, and he asked her if she'd be willing to give him a few refresher riding lessons. "I learned to ride, but I haven't in a few years, and I'd like to exercise the farm's horses."

"I have a group lesson tomorrow afternoon. Why don't you join us? I'd be happy to have you." Her offer, along with her smile, felt genuine.

"Thanks, I'd like that."

"Good. I'll see you at two." People began arriving, and Len excused himself and went into the tack room to straighten up before heading to the hayloft. Opening one of the trap doors in the hayloft floor, he began retrieving bales of hay and dropping them through the door.

"Don't you ever question me in front of the other men!" Len turned around to meet Cliff's wrathful stare.

Len wasn't about to back down. "Then don't be a complete ass!" Len almost smiled when he saw the surprised look on Cliff's face. Defiance was obviously not what he'd been expecting. "Fred and Randy have been keeping this farm going for the last year with very little help from you, and they know what needs to be done. And they most certainly don't deserve to be ordered around like children!" Cliff's eyes were fierce as he stepped closer. "You may own this farm, but you're not the King of—"

Len was taken completely off guard when Cliff kissed him and kissed him hard. Damn, that felt good, and Len felt his indignation slip away as Cliff's lips assaulted his, teeth lightly scraping over his lower lip.

Hands wound around Len's waist, pulling their bodies together. Len ran his hands down Cliff's back, cupping his butt and holding him still, thrusting his hips forward as he ground himself against him. Len closed his eyes as pressure built at the base of his spine, and slowly he began to ease the pressure on Cliff's body and lips. If he didn't, he knew he was going to be a mess for the rest of the day.

Cliff stepped back, looking into Len's eyes.

Len shook his head to clear it. "—Siam. These guys love the farm as much as you do."

Cliff held up his hand in surrender. "Jesus, I thought kissing you would shut you up."

"Nope. It's going to take a lot more than a kiss." Len winked and smiled. "Seriously, they've been taking care of the farm while you've been grieving and taking care of Geoff. They've really stepped up."

"If I tell you you're right, will you shut up and kiss me?" Cliff grabbed Len by the belt loop and yanked him forward, crashing their lips together again. Len nodded against Cliff's lips, and this time all his thoughts, except those about how Cliff's lips made him feel, flew from his head, and he whimpered softly against Cliff's lips, the heat from Cliff's body seeping through his clothes.

Cliff pulled his head back but kept their bodies close. "Dad always said I was a bull in a china shop when it came to the farmhands."

Len didn't try to pull away. "Seems to me your dad was right." Len didn't want to let go. He liked, really liked, how it felt to hold Cliff. "We have to be careful." Len looked toward the stairs and slowly moved away, breaking their contact.

"I know." Len saw Cliff swallow and look down toward the floor. "I should be going."

Len wasn't sure what to make of Cliff's sudden reluctance and shyness, but he nodded and watched as he descended the stairs. Had he hurt Cliff's feelings? Jesus, he hadn't meant to. He just meant that they needed to be discreet, and kissing in the hayloft probably wasn't the smartest thing. Len let his thoughts swirl as he finished getting the hay and closed the trap door. God, he wished he had someone to talk to. But the one person he'd always been able to talk to was Ruby, and she was gone. Len stopped at the top of the stairs. "Shit. That has to be part of it." He just needed to figure out how to broach the subject.

Len slowly descended the stairs. The hay had landed in a pile in the middle aisle of the barn, and Len stacked it near the stalls for easy retrieval.

Love Means ... *Courage*

"Len." He looked up and saw Fred walking through the barn. "Is everything okay? Cliff just stopped me and told me I was right, and that we should plant this afternoon."

"You were right." Len said, matter-of-fact.

"It's just that Cliff never changes him mind."

Len shrugged and changed the subject. "He did this time."

"You about done here?" Len nodded and looked around to make sure. "Then let's go check out those last fields, make sure we've got everything we need. It's supposed to rain again tonight, and we need to get the last of the planting done."

"Okay, give me ten minutes."

"Meet you at my truck." Fred walked toward the equipment shed, and Len made sure everything was shut before meeting Fred at his truck. They both climbed in and headed toward the former Henderson farm. "Len, can I ask you something?"

Len turned toward Fred. "Sure."

"What's going on between you and Cliff?"

"Who says anything's going on?"

"No one, but I've seen the way he looks at you and the way you look at him." Fred blew out his breath. "Cliff loved Ruby, but he never looked at her the way he looks at you, especially when you're looking the other way. And, I've seen you giving him the same looks." Len peered out the window, unsure whether to say anything at all. "You don't have to answer me, but I wanted you to know that it's cool." Len's head snapped around to look at Fred. Had he heard right? Len stammered unintelligibly, his gut clenching, and he thought he was going to be sick.

Fred pulled the truck off the road near one of the fields, and Len breathed deeply, trying to drive down this sick feeling. "I've known Cliff for almost ten years, and I've seen that boy go through hell. He won't admit it to anyone out loud, but I know he's not really into girls. I was sort of shocked when he fell in love with Ruby, but he did, and they were happy."

Len could hardly believe his ears. "You... you're okay with that?"

"Yeah, and I think Randy is too. So neither you nor Cliff has anything to worry about from us. Unless you hurt him. That's boy's been through an awful lot. His daddy was a good man, but he could be as closed-minded as they come, and he wasn't shy about expressing his views, if you know what I mean." Fred shut off the engine and opened his door, getting out of the truck.

Len followed suit and didn't know what to say at all but decided to go for the most obvious. "Thanks."

"You're welcome. Now let's figure out if we can get these fields planted." Together they walked down the embankment and onto the tilled earth. "This seems pretty firm. We shouldn't have any trouble getting in here today."

"Good. Let's get the tractor set and get these planted so the rain can do its job." They got back in the truck, and after stopping at one other place, drove back to the farm. After eating his lunch, Len started the tractor and drove it to the fields, spending the rest of the day planting the last acreage. As he pulled back into the drive that evening, it was nearly dark. He put the tractor in the shed and covered the attached planter with a tarp.

The farm was quiet, and no one else appeared to be around. Len looked toward the house and saw Cliff standing in one of the windows. "Patience, Len. You've got to have patience." He waved, and Cliff waved back. Len then got in his car and headed for home.

Love Means ... Courage

CHAPTER 10

"MAKE sure you keep your feet down." Nicole was standing in the middle of the ring, calling to her students. "Look at Len; his are perfect."

Len smiled to himself. He hadn't been on a horse in almost three years, but it had all come flooding back as soon as he'd thrown his leg over Misty's back. *Yes, I definitely have to do this more often.*

"You're all doing very well. Now let's bring them to a trot, and remember to match your rhythm to your horse's." Len leaned forward, and Misty began trotting. He easily matched her rhythm, and they trotted around the ring. "You're doing great, Len." Nicole called as he passed. "Just a few more minutes." They continued trotting until Nicole called a halt and had them dismount before walking their horses around the ring to cool them off.

"Wen!" He knew that voice. Looking toward the barn, he saw Cliff holding Geoff on his shoulders, the little guy pointing. Len smiled and walked Misty over. "Hossey wide."

"He's been watching you for the past half hour," Cliff said.

Love Means ... *Courage*

Len remounted Misty, and Cliff handed Geoff to him. Nicole took the reins and walked Misty and her two riders around the ring. Geoff laughed and squealed as they rode. Every now and then, he'd pat her neck. "Good hossey." Two times around the ring was enough, and Len handed Geoff back to Cliff and dismounted.

Walking Misty out of the ring, Len led her back to her stall, took off her saddle and blanket, and gave the good girl a brush down.

"You ride really well." Cliff and Geoff peered over the stall door as Len finished up. "Maybe we could go riding in the morning?"

"I'd like that, but who's going to watch Geoff?" He leaned over and tickled the little one in question.

Cliff shifted Geoff and blew a raspberry on his tummy. "Aunt Mari's coming over tomorrow morning; she needs some time away from Aunt Janelle." He spoke to Geoff in that sing-songy voice, but the words were for Len.

"Speaking of Janelle, she and I are going to the musical at the high school on Friday. Would you and Geoffy here want to go along?" he asked, as he tickled that little belly and earned a giggle. Len finished with Misty and left the stall, closing the door behind him. "I'm just meeting her at the school for the play." Cliff gave him a funny look. "Cliff, we're just friends, nothing more."

"Oh, I believe you. It's her thoughts on the subject I'm worried about." Len knew that Cliff was making more out of his friendship with Janelle than there was. "It would be fun to get out of the house for a while."

Len couldn't keep the smile off his face, no matter how hard he tried. "Good." Len didn't want to turn away but knew he had to. There was work to be done, and it wasn't going to get done on its own.

"I'm trying to put together some projects for the farm, and I was wondering if you'd be willing to go over them with me. Hopefully I'll have them done today. I could sure use your help making sure I haven't forgotten anything."

"Be happy to. Maybe after our ride tomorrow?" He felt his stomach doing little flip-flops. Maybe they'd get to do more than look at the accounts. His attention zeroed in on Cliff's lips. God, he wanted to taste them again. He could remember every detail of the kiss in the hayloft the day before, and he really wanted a repeat, maybe on the ride tomorrow. Len suppressed a quiver of excitement. Maybe they'd do more during their ride tomorrow.

"Sure." They stood in the barn, smiling at each other like idiots, neither of them breaking eye contact. Brisk footsteps at the door broke the spell, and they both turned to see Fred striding in the barn. Cliff's expression shifted quickly, and to Len he looked like a kid caught with his hand in the cookie jar. Without a word to either of them, he quickly left the barn.

"You about done for the day?"

"Yeah." Len saw Fred's knowing expression and tried to wipe the hopeful expectation off his face.

"Randy and I are as well. We thought we'd head into town for a beer. Wanna join us? Randy mentioned Steve's, which means Shell's working and he wants to see her."

"Sounds good. I'll just need to stop back here on the way home so I can bring in the horses. It's supposed to get cool tonight, and I don't want them out."

"Then you can ride with me, and I'll drop you off later." Len nodded and did one last visual inspection before following Fred to his truck.

Love Means ... Courage

LEN arrived at the farm, extra early. The sun was barely peeking over the horizon when he opened the barn door. The morning was chilly, but according to the radio, it was going to be a sunny day. Len let the horses out into the pastures, leaving Misty and Thunder in the barn. Fred had told him discreetly at the bar the night before that Thunder was the horse that Cliff liked to ride. After spot-cleaning the stalls, he emptied the wheelbarrow and began brushing the horses.

As he was getting the saddles ready, he heard a car pull into the drive and figured it was Nicole. A few minutes later, he heard heavy footsteps approaching. "Cliff?"

"Yeah, it's me."

Len felt the excited flutter he'd been keeping under control flare to life. "I've got Thunder brushed; you just need to saddle him."

"Thanks." Len saw Cliff walk by Misty's stall, glancing inside on his way to the tack room, returning with an armload of tack. Len finished brushing Misty and left the stall to get her tack.

It didn't take long for him to get her saddled and ready, and Len walked Misty out of the barn, meeting Cliff and Thunder in the yard. "Did you have a place in mind for our ride?" Len patted Misty as he looked over at Cliff, who was already mounting Thunder, and Len got an eyeful of a tight butt encased in a pair of jeans.

"Yeah. There's a place I'd like to show you, if that's okay."

Len mounted, the leather creaking as he settled in the saddle. "Lead on; we'll follow."

Cliff headed around the pasture and across the field near the barn with Len following behind. The sun quickly warmed the air as they rode. At the edge of the field, the terrain gave way to large trees and thick undergrowth. Cliff led them along a path through the trees. "When I was a kid, I used to ride this trail all the time." Cliff slowed his horse so Len and Misty could get closer. "In the summer, there's nothing like the cool air beneath these trees." They kept to the trail, which was distinct but looked like it hadn't been used much lately. "There's a creek up ahead. It should be all right, but take it easy just in case."

Len heard the moving water before he saw it, and Cliff made a right turn, following the trail on the small bluff overlooking the creek. "In the summer, this was where we'd play when we needed to cool off." Cliff smiled and returned his attention to the trail ahead of him. "It isn't too far ahead." Len had no idea when Cliff was referring to, but he nodded and followed.

The trees gave way to a small meadowed clearing along the creek. Cliff rode to the center and then dismounted, and Len did the same. Cliff tied each of the horses to a tree and pulled the blanket from the back of his saddle, spreading it on the ground and motioning for Len to have a seat.

Cliff sat next to him, turning so they could look at each other. He thought Cliff had something he wanted to talk about, but instead he leaned forward and brought their lips together tentatively. Len slid his hand over Cliff's cheek and deepened the kiss, allowing himself to get a good, full taste of Cliff's mouth. That earned him a small moan, and he slid his fingers into Cliff's soft hair while his other hand slid along Cliff's jeans-encased leg.

Cliff pulled back slightly. "Len, I don't know what to do… I mean with…."

Len saw Cliff swallow hard, and Len took control, bringing their lips together again as he shifted on the blanket. His jeans were way too tight and getting tighter by the second. Cliff had his body in high gear. Using his weight, he shifted Cliff backward, settling him on the blanket as he continued to feast on Cliff's glorious mouth. He felt Cliff's hands on his back, stroking him over his shirt, and he slipped a hand under Cliff's—smooth, soft skin beneath his palm.

He could feel Cliff's excitement against his hip as their bodies ground together slowly, their kissing setting the tempo. This was what Len had been hoping for, wanting, and waiting to have happen for what seemed like forever. Cliff was here in his arms, kissing him, and he could feel his skin beneath his hands, smooth and hot, scaldingly hot against him. And he wanted even more. His feverish, passion-filled mind wanted to feel Cliff against him, his hot skin sliding over his.

"I've wanted this, wanted you forever." Len looked into Cliff's eyes, about to take his mouth again, but what he saw made him stop, and he slowly lifted himself up, giving Cliff space. "Are you okay?"

Cliff couldn't meet his eyes. "Yes."

Len knew Cliff was lying, probably to spare his feelings, but he'd seen that look many times. He knew that look intimately. After all, he'd seen it reflected back at him in the mirror so many times. The G-word. The dreaded G-word that had haunted him daily until he'd met Tim. Guilt had eaten him alive until he'd finally come to grips with who he was, and he could see those same feelings, that same look, in Cliff's eyes.

Cliff stifled a groan and sat back on the blanket, helping Len to a seated position. "Why'd you stop? Don't you want to?"

As Cliff began to get up, Len put his hand on his thigh. "Of course. I want to strip you bare and feel every glorious, sexy inch of you. Run my hands over you and taste every inch of you until you beg me to stop. I want to kiss you, feel you, hold you, and see what you look like when you can't hold back any more." The words tumbled out of him before he could stop them, and he wouldn't take them back no matter what. Len sat back and waited for Cliff's reaction, half expecting that he'd scared the man off.

"I feel so ashamed of myself. You feel good, and you make me feel good, but these thoughts won't go away no matter how hard I try."

"What thoughts?"

The sigh seemed to deflate him. "That I'm being unfaithful to Ruby."

A tickle of sadness scratched at his throat. "You know she was my friend. The best friend I ever had."

"Did she know? Did you ever tell her?"

Len nodded. "She did know, and I didn't tell her; she told me. At your wedding while I was dancing with her. She told me to find someone who would make me happy." He ran his fingertips over Cliff's cheek, leaving the rest unspoken.

Cliff whispered almost to himself. "She never said anything."

"She promised she'd respect my privacy, and that was one thing about her, she never broke a confidence. Once she made a promise to keep something secret, the CIA couldn't have dragged it out of her." Len smiled, remembering his friend.

Cliff smiled too, but it soon faded. "I loved her very much, but there was always this part of me that needed something else. I never told her and did my best to deny it even to myself because I didn't want to hurt her or get hurt myself. But something that I couldn't describe was always missing, and I feel so guilty...." He swallowed, and Len gave him a minute to get hold of his feelings.

"She knew you loved her, and you made her happy. The day she told me she was pregnant, and then when I saw her with Geoff, those were the happiest I ever saw her."

Cliff swallowed hard. "But what would she feel about this, me—us?"

Love Means ... *Courage*

Len was quiet, thinking how he could best answer a question that no one could answer, not now. "Cliff, she knows now, and I know how I think she feels, but I can't answer that question for you. That's one thing you have to answer for yourself. But the one thing I can tell you is that she always, always, always wanted me to be happy, and I know she wants the same for you." Len looked into Cliff's sad, confused, conflicted eyes. "When you were married, you were faithful to her?" Cliff nodded. "You loved her?"

Cliff nodded again. "But—"

"You gave her all the love you had, and that's all anyone can ever ask for." Slowly, Len got to his feet and stood by the edge of the blanket. He wanted to kiss that look off Cliff's face, but he was afraid it would only add to his confusion. He needed to give Cliff time to decide how he felt. Oh, he probably could have nestled Cliff back on the blanket and made him forget what he was feeling for a while in a lust-induced haze, but that was not what he wanted. He didn't want Cliff's lust; he wanted his passion and love. Extending his hand, he helped Cliff to his feet. "We should probably get back." Cliff bent down to fold up the blanket, and Len turned to untie Misty. "I waited almost five years for you to kiss me again; I can wait a little longer for—"

"Did you say something?" Cliff asked.

The leather creaked as Len mounted, hiding his huff of annoyance. "No." Cliff mounted as well, and they rode quietly back to the farm, both of them deep in thought.

At the barn, Len unsaddled Misty and put her in a pasture while Cliff unsaddled Thunder. "I'll meet you inside in a few minutes." Len must have given him a confused look because Cliff continued, "Remember, you promised to help me with the projections?"

"I remember. I'll finish up here and be right in."

Cliff stopped and looked at Len. He even opened his mouth to say something, but stopped and turned, walking out of the barn. Len wondered what Cliff was about to say as he watched him leave. Shaking his head, he got Thunder settled before leaving the barn himself.

Len knocked on the back door and then opened it, slipping off his boots and walking into the kitchen.

"Hi, Len."

"Hi, Mari. How's work going? I was surprised you had the day off."

She smiled back at him. "I had a vacation day to use, and Cliff said he needed some help. The kids are excited about summer vacation, and I figured they could torture a substitute for a day." She grinned and turned back to the sink. "Cliff's in the office."

Len looked around, wondering where Geoff was. "Thanks." He went through the living room and knocked on the door frame. Geoff was playing on the office floor, and Cliff was scowling over the papers he was working on.

"Hi, Wen."

"Hi, Geoff. Oof." He humphed as a small body plowed into him.

Cliff looked up from his papers, still scowling. "Geoff, please go find Aunt Mari."

"Okay, Daddy." Geoff let go of Len and ran out of the office. A few seconds later he heard giggles and laughter from the kitchen.

"What can I help you with, Cliff?"

The scowl stayed in place. "Shut the door." Len complied, and Cliff handed him a piece of paper filled with expenses and their descriptions. "I've looked this over a dozen times, and I can't find a mistake."

"Should there be one?"

"God, I hope so, because if there isn't then I need to come up with another ten thousand dollars in order to make it until harvest. The last year wiped out all my savings as well as the available cash in the farm accounts. I just wish I'd known about the Henderson place last year. I've even taken into account the increased revenue from the horses, but it still isn't enough."

Len's first instinct was to try to reassure Cliff, but instead, he sat in one of the chairs and began reviewing the figures line by line, but he couldn't find anything wrong. All the estimates seemed reasonable and the expenses necessary. "Let's go over each item, both income and expenses, and we'll talk them through. Maybe something will come to mind.

Cliff nodded and Len pulled up a chair to the desk. Together they went through every item, scrutinizing each expense or revenue. They found where Cliff had made a mistake in estimating the fuel, but that was offset because he forgot to add in the cost of tractor maintenance. In the end, they were right back where they started. "So the expenses are accurate, and the revenues won't change until fall. What can we do to bring in more money?" A knock at the door interrupted Len's thought.

Mari poked her head inside. "Lunch will be ready in an hour, and I have to be downtown at one."

"Thanks, Mari." Cliff replied absently as he pondered over the figures. "We've put everything to work we can find."

"Is there anything you could sell to raise the money?"

"There is one thing, but it's not very realistic. When dad bought the Henderson place, he bought everything, including the house. I was thinking that we could sell it, but that could take months, and with mortgage interest rates sky high, who'd be able to afford it anyway? The only way dad was able to borrow the money to buy the place was through a subsidized loan to help family farms."

"You're going to sell the Henderson place?" Both Len and Cliff turned to Mari, looking guilty because they'd forgotten she was there.

"I was thinking about it, why?"

"Janelle's driving me crazy, and I was going to ask if I could live there. It's not very big, and I could fix it up."

Len looked at her, an idea forming. "Better yet, you could buy it." Both Cliff and Mari looked at Len like he was nuts. "Hear me out. The barn isn't near the house, so you could carve out a lot that contains the farmhouse and a nice yard."

Mari smiled slightly. "I know the house, and it's nice, but how could I afford a mortgage?"

Len looked at both Mari and Cliff. "You don't need one. Cliff could sell it to you on a land contract. You pay him the down payment, and he writes a land contract for the balance. Instead of making payments to the bank, you pay Cliff. The interest rate is nine percent instead of the sixteen the bank is charging. Cliff gets the cash he needs, and you get a house of your own." Both Cliff and Mari looked at each other, and Len noticed the first glimmer of hope. "You'd need a lawyer to help with the contract, and I'd hire someone to appraise the house to make sure the selling price is fair, and you're all set."

"I have the money from Dad's life insurance. I was going to offer to lend it to you, but this is even better. I could get my own house, and you'd reduce some of your own expenses and have additional money coming in each month, plus you'd get the money you need without borrowing."

Len sat back in the chair, smiling to himself as Cliff and his sister started talking about the arrangements and what was possible. They were both so excited that neither of them saw him leave the office. He found Geoff in the living room playing with his trucks. After waving goodbye to the boy, he put his boots back on and headed back to work. There were always stalls to clean.

Len got the wheelbarrow and started cleaning one of the stalls. "Len." He jumped when he heard the voice behind him. "Sorry, didn't mean to startle you, but I wanted to ask you to join us for lunch, and tell you thank you." Cliff stepped into the stall. "I can't believe you've only been here a month—I didn't think things would ever be going so well again." Cliff stepped to him and kissed him, their lips gently exploring. Cliff pulled back, smiling. "See you in fifteen for lunch."

Len nodded, smiling as well.

CHAPTER 11

"HEY, Mom. Would you like to go to the play?" He'd just gotten home and was rushing through the house to get cleaned up and ready. "It starts at seven-thirty, and we're meeting Cliff and Geoff at the Dairy Barn for dinner."

She turned around in her chair. "I don't know."

"What are you going to do, watch television all evening? Come on, it'll be fun." Len was already halfway toward the bathroom.

"How dressy should I get?" He could hear her walking toward her bedroom.

"We're going to the Dairy Barn and the high school. Dress comfortably." She laughed, and he grabbed his clothes before stepping in the bathroom. Len started the water and stepped under the spray. He was happy and felt like singing. He washed quickly and got out, toweling himself off before going to the sink and shaving. He really wanted to look nice. God, it felt like he was back in high school, except back then, he'd never been this nervous. Washing off the remaining shaving cream, he combed his hair, parting it in the middle. Then he pulled on his pants and shirt, and he found himself actually turning around to look at his butt in the mirror. "I'm turning into a girl," he told himself, but he still looked to make sure the pants looked good. Then he padded to his bedroom to finish dressing.

When he was done, he walked to the living room. His mother was already set, sitting on the sofa waiting as Len checked his watch.

"Do I look okay?"

"You look great, Mom." She really did. "Shall we go?" He handed his mom her jacket, and they left the house, locking the door behind them. Len held the door for her, got in the car, and they headed for town.

The Dairy Barn parking lot was full, and Len just managed to find a place to park. Luckily, when they got inside, Cliff and Geoff were already there with Geoff standing on the seat, watching for them. He began jumping up and down when he saw them. "Wen!" Before Cliff could stop him, he'd jumped off the seat and went running, and Len scooped him up to high-pitched giggles. He carried him over to the table, setting him in the seat next to Cliff.

"Cliff, this is my mother."

Cliff extended his hand. "It's nice to meet you, Mrs. Parker."

"Please, call me Lorna, and it's nice to meet you."

"And this—" he tickled Geoff's tummy, "—giggle monster is Geoff."

They sat down, and the waitress brought menus and took their drink orders. "What do you want, Geoff?" Len asked as Geoff played with his silverware.

"Bwench Bwies."

Cliff sat him down and took away the silverware. "You can have french fries, but only if you sit down and behave." Geoff sat in his booster seat, his head swiveling all around the restaurant. The waitress returned and passed out the drinks before taking their orders and rushing away to the next table.

"You look familiar, Lorna, where do you work?"

"I work at the hospital in medical records, but I've seen you and Geoff in the grocery store a few times."

"I suppose in a town like this, everyone seems familiar."

"So how are things at the farm?"

Cliff smiled, and Len thought how wonderful he looked when he smiled. "Going much better. My dad bought the Henderson farm just before he died, and my sister has decided to buy the house. We met with the lawyer today, and he's drawing up the paperwork to subdivide the land and complete the purchase. He said everything should be done in a month or so." The relaxed look on Cliff's face was like a breath of fresh air. Len hadn't seen that before, and he couldn't help smiling back, knowing he'd helped put that smile on Cliff's face.

The waitress returned with their food and set their plates in front of them. "Can I get you anything else?"

Cliff was already eating, so Len answered. "No, thank you." She smiled, and then she was off again. "Man, they're hopping tonight."

Cliff gave Geoff some fries, and he started shoving them in his mouth one right after the other until he looked like a chipmunk. "Swallow before you eat any more," Cliff instructed.

Len looked at his mother, and they smiled at each other and continued eating. When they were finished, the waitress brought the check, and Len scooped it up before Cliff had a chance, excusing himself and heading to the register. He was next in line to pay when he heard, "What do you think you're doing?"

Len turned around and looked Cliff in the eye. "Buying dinner. You've fed me enough over the last few weeks; it's just my turn." Len paid the bill at the register and met them back at the table. He noticed that Cliff had left the tip, and they gathered their things and left the restaurant, getting in their cars and driving the stone's throw to the high school.

THEY met up again just outside the gymnasium that had been converted into an auditorium. "Evening, Len." Janelle approached when she saw him, smiling brightly. He noticed that her smile faded slightly when she saw that he wasn't alone.

"Hi, Janelle." He introduced his mother, bought the tickets, and the group filed inside. The gymnasium/auditorium looked almost exactly like it had for the production of *Grease* five years earlier. When they got to an empty aisle they filed in and took their seats, much to Geoff's consternation. He insisted on rearranging the seating so he sat between his daddy and Len. Janelle seemed slightly put out, but Len noticed that his mother looked rather pleased. Before too much could be said, the lights dimmed, and the orchestra began the overture.

Len helped keep an eye on Geoff, who seemed to enjoy the music. Len had thought he'd fall asleep, but Geoff spent much of the first act listening to the music and watching the actors in their brightly colored costumes.

At intermission, Len excused himself and returned with drinks and some crackers for Geoff. As he returned, he saw Janelle and Cliff talking together. They broke apart as he approached, but Len could see the set of her face and knew that she wasn't happy about what had been said. "I've got drinks." He handed one to Cliff, Janelle, and his mother, "And I got you some cheesy crackers." Geoff took the package, and Cliff got a sippy cup out of the bag.

The lights dimmed, and the second act began. Cliff put away what was left of the crackers, and Geoff settled on his lap, almost immediately going to sleep. Awhile later, as the play progressed, Cliff signaled that he needed to get up, so Len took Geoff. The youngster slipped his arms around Len's neck and rested his head on his shoulder, immediately falling back to sleep. Len moved over a seat so Geoff's feet wouldn't lay on Janelle's dress. Cliff returned, sat back down, and smiled at Len, who returned his attention to the play. But his attention didn't remain there. A few minutes later, he felt the light touch of Cliff's hand on his. He looked over and saw Cliff's smile in the darkness. His skin felt so warm and so good, the touch so welcome and normal. It didn't stay long, but it gave Len a warm feeling inside just the same.

At the end of the play, everyone applauded, and the lights came back up. Geoff stirred, and Len handed him back to his father, and they filed out. "Thank you, Len. I had a nice time." Janelle sounded normal, but her face was still set.

"I did too."

She smiled and then joined the crowd exiting the school before Len could offer to walk her to her car.

"It's okay, Len." He felt a hand on his shoulder. "She'll be fine." He turned and saw Cliff still holding Geoff. "I need to get him home. I'll see you tomorrow for our morning ride." Len and Lorna followed Cliff to his car and helped him get Geoff settled before walking to their own vehicle and heading home.

"You know Janelle has feelings for you," Lorna commented as they drove.

Len didn't look away from the road. "We're just friends."

Love Means ... *Courage*

"Maybe you are, but she isn't. I think her brother tried to set her straight, and that's why she was so cold the rest of the evening." He felt her hand pat his arm. "If I were you, I'd keep my distance for a while. She might get the message." Len nodded and drove, but he didn't want to think about Janelle. Instead, his thoughts kept focusing on the feel of a certain hand against his.

THE horses were saddled and ready to go when Len arrived at the barn the following morning. "You usually have them ready for me, so I thought I'd return the favor. Besides, Mari stopped by last night and asked to use the guest room until Janelle calms down."

"Does this have to do with your conversation last night?"

"Yes." Cliff checked to make sure no one was around. "I don't really want to talk about Janelle, okay?"

Len nodded, and they mounted. "Where are we going today?"

"I thought we'd go back to the clearing by the creek." Cliff gave his horse a flick, and Thunder took off. They raced over the pasture, Cliff laughing and calling back to Len. He didn't feel as comfortable as Cliff did, so he and Misty cantered across the field, catching up at the far side just before the trees.

The sun shone through the canopy, creating dappled shade, quickly warming the air even under the trees as they rode toward the creek. The familiar sound of the water greeted them as they turned and followed the creek. They didn't talk as they rode, which Len didn't find uncomfortable or unusual, but he did notice that a blanket was attached to the back of Cliff's saddle. At the clearing, they dismounted, and Len tied up the horses so they could graze while Cliff spread the blanket on the soft grass.

Cliff sat on the blanket, and Len joined him. He suspected that Cliff wanted to talk, but instead he put those lips that so fascinated Len to better use and kissed him. Cliff's fingers wound into Len's hair, and he felt Cliff press his weight against him, settling him back on the blanket. "Are you sure?"

Len felt the buttons of his shirt being undone. "Very sure. I've been wondering for days how Ruby would feel about this, and last night I got my answer." The last of Len's shirt buttons were undone, and warm hands stroked along his chest.

Len arched into the touch, aching to feel those hands on his skin. "How?" He began opening Cliff's shirt, but he gently stilled his hands before working a nipple between work-roughened fingers, and Len hissed into the sensation.

"All I have left of her is Geoff, and he loves you." Cliff leaned forward, nibbling gently at the base of Len's neck. "Besides, I know she'd want me to be happy, and you make me happy."

There were so many questions he wanted to ask, but they flew from his mind as Cliff captured his lips. Concerns, questions, rational thought—all stopped as he was kissed within an inch of his life. Their tongues swirled around each other as Len felt Cliff's weight rest on top of him. This time, he wound his arms around him, his hands settling on Cliff's firm butt.

"I'm glad, because you make me happy too." *God, did he ever*!

Len slid his hands beneath Cliff's shirt, firm back muscles sliding beneath his fingers and palms. Cliff lifted his head, and Len slid the shirt up Cliff's body before pulling it over his head and off his arms. He nearly came when he first felt the skin of Cliff's chest against his own. This was what he'd been dreaming about for so long: lips kissing, chests sliding together. Len had always thought he'd die if he got to feel Cliff like this, but now that he was, it wasn't enough. He wanted more, needed more, and he let his hands take it, sliding them down Cliff's back, into his jeans, and along that smooth, firm butt.

"Len." It sounded like a plea, and he answered it by massaging Cliff's butt as they continued their passionate kissing.

A steady stream of little sounds reached Len's ears, sounding like music—passionate, thrilling, love music. Slowly, he pulled his hands from Cliff's pants and rolled their bodies on the blanket. Now Cliff was beneath him, all that skin laid out for him. "You're beautiful, more beautiful than I ever imagined, and I imagined a lot." Len lowered his head, capturing a pink nipple between his lips. "I dreamed what you'd look like, what you'd taste like." His tongue swirled around the pointed, hard bud. "What you'd sound like."

Cliff moaned softly, and Len smiled. He slipped off his shirt and returned his attention and his hands to Cliff, sliding them over the bulge in the front of Cliff's pants. "Len, I can't...."

Taking pity on him, Len opened Cliff's pants and pushed them down, sliding his hands over the hard shaft. He watched as Cliff's stomach muscles clenched and his breathing became ragged. "So close," Cliff moaned.

Len continued working Cliff's hot shaft as he leaned close to his ear. "Let it go; give it all to me." A long, ragged cry echoed through the clearing as Cliff did just that, coming over Len's hand and onto his stomach. Then Len watched as his head rested back on the blanket, and his body relaxed. "That was beautiful. I loved the way your eyes locked onto mine when you came."

Cliff leaned forward, and Len brought their lips together, thrilled he could put that happy, sated look on Cliff's face. While they kissed, he felt Cliff's hands opening his pants before tentatively reaching his hand inside, and shortly after he felt the air and Cliff's light touch on him, like he wasn't sure.

"Just do what *you* like," Len whispered. Slowly, Cliff's hand began to move, sending electric shocks up and down Len's spine. Len was already so keyed up, he knew he wasn't going to last long, and he didn't, throwing his head back as his climax slammed into him, taking his breath away. "Cliff!"

When his vision cleared, Len settled on the blanket, gulping air like a sprinter. They lay together, facing each other, hands entwined and lips pressed to each others. No words were used—none were needed—as they basked in a heady afterglow. It was only the sound of the horses whickering that brought them back to the present. Cliff huffed softly. "We should get back." But it was obvious his heart wasn't in it. His heart was right here.

Len returned the slight sigh. "I know. I've got work to do, and I wouldn't want my boss to think I was shirking my duties." He smirked, and Cliff bopped him on the arm. "But I just want to stay here with you too."

That led to another round of kissing and touching, which in turn led to some more rolling around on the blanket. Finally, Len sat up, his eyes and hands resting on Cliff's body. "We really should get back. Damn it." Slowly, he got to his feet, pants around his ankles, shirt strewn somewhere. Cliff was in worse shape; his pants were hanging in some bushes. They both laughed at their exuberance and retrieved their clothing.

Cliff used a corner of the blanket to clean them up, and after getting dressed, they rolled up the blanket and untied the horses. Before mounting their rides, Len gave Cliff another kiss, and they headed back to the farm, riding back through the woods grinning from ear to ear.

CHAPTER 12

"ACCORDING to The Andersons of Maumee, Ohio, corn was up ten cents a bushel, settling at two-forty on fears of a sustained drought in the plains and Midwest." The announcer went on to give the rest of the farm commodity prices as Len drove to the farm. "The weather today should be partly cloudy with a chance of a pop-up thunderstorm."

"You've said that for the last week, and nothing!" Len switched off the radio in disgust as he pulled into the drive in front of the barn and parked his car. Cliff came out of the house with Geoff right behind him.

"Son of a bitch, I wish it would rain. They keep calling for freaking thundershowers and nothing comes!" Cliff's temper was definitely up, and while Len knew a few things he could do to turn the grumpy bear into a whimpering pile of JELL-O, they hadn't had much of a chance lately. For the past few weeks, they'd gone riding together a few mornings a week and always to the clearing, which Len was beginning to think of as *their* clearing. But there hadn't been anyone to watch Geoff, so they hadn't been able to enjoy a morning ride for the last week, and with the lack of rain, Cliff had been getting grumpier and snappier.

As Cliff approached, Len saw Geoff trip on something in the grass.

"Son of a bitch!" The high-pitched tone rang out, clear as a bell.

Len saw Cliff's head snap around to glare at Geoff, and Len put his hand on Cliff's arm as he used the over to cover his mouth to keep from laughing. Cliff yanked Geoff to his feet, looking like he was going to spank him. "Don't, Cliff. He doesn't know what he said. He just repeated what he heard you say not two seconds ago."

The glare he got would melt concrete. "If I had said that in front of my parents, they'd have washed my mouth out with soap."

Len raised his eyebrows. "Didn't help with *your* potty mouth, did it?" Finally, Cliff smiled and set Geoff back on his feet. "What's got you in such a foul mood anyway?"

"I'm just worried." Every farmer worried about things. Len knew that. After all, they were at the mercy of something as uncontrollable as the weather.

"I know. But it has only been a little over a week, and I have a good feeling we're going to get some rain soon." From the look on Cliff's face, he wasn't buying it. Len looked again at Geoff, making sure he was occupied; the boy had climbed into his sandbox and was already playing happily. "Come on. I have something to show you." Len led Cliff through the barn and into the tack room, pulling him inside and shutting the door. As soon as he heard the click of the latch, he took Cliff's face in his hands and kissed him hard.

"Len, we can't. Not here." There was no strength in his voice, and Len pressed his advantage, sliding his tongue along the ridge of Cliff's lip, earning himself a soft whimper. "I've missed that."

"So have I," Len said as he pulled Cliff into a tight embrace, doing his best to kiss him breathless. "Let's plan on a ride this afternoon. I think we could both use it." Cliff nodded, unable to form words as he ran his tongue over his kiss-swollen lips. "Mari said yesterday that she'd be able to watch Geoff for a few hours."

The surprised look on Cliff's face was precious. "You asked her?"

"She volunteered—said a ride would be good for you." Len released Cliff and opened the tack room door, watching a smiling Cliff as he walked back to where Geoff was playing.

Len went to work but was having trouble concentrating. His thoughts kept returning to Cliff. They'd been seeing each other, sort of, for the past few weeks, but they rarely talked about anything other than the farm. Len was hoping that Cliff felt something for him and that this wasn't just about sex. He didn't think it was, but Cliff didn't talk about his feelings, and when he did, they were generally ones he yelled about.

"Hey, Len. Morning." He turned his head and saw Randy standing by the stall he was cleaning. "Where were you? I called a couple times, but you didn't answer."

"Sorry." He hadn't realized he'd been that preoccupied.

"Looks like it's going to be a hot one." He looked toward the barn door. "Sure hope we get some rain." The topic of rain was on everyone's mind.

"They're calling for a chance of showers, but they've done that every day this week." Len wiped his brow, more out of frustration than sweat. "With the rising price of corn and the drought in the plains, the farm would clean up if we brought in a good harvest." Len knew that would go a long way toward easing Cliff's fears and help calm his prickly mood.

"If you need me, holler. I'm going to check on the cattle, make sure they have enough water. Fred's off today."

Len smiled and nodded. "And you do the same." He got back to work, loading muck from the stalls into the wheelbarrow.

"Len." He jumped a mile when he heard the voice behind him. Why was everyone sneaking up on him today?

"Hi, Janelle." He suppressed a groan. She'd taken to stopping by the farm to talk when he had work to do, and the attention was becoming less and less welcome. "How are you?" He kept his voice pleasant. She was his friend, after all, but he was finally beginning to see that Cliff had been right, and that she had feelings for him that went beyond friendship.

"I'm fine. I was at the store this morning and saw a notice that Ludington was having a summer festival. I know it's one of their tourist things, but it might be fun, and I thought we could go. I know Cliff will give you the time off."

"I can't." He smiled; for once he really did have other plans. "Cliff is taking Geoff to the beach, and I promised I'd go along." There was no way he was breaking a promise to Geoffy. He'd been so cute when he'd asked; there was no way he'd have turned him down. *Wen, will you go to the beach wiff us?*

"You'd rather go to the beach with a two-year-old than go out with me?" She looked mad enough to spit nails.

Len set his pitchfork against the wall of the stall and turned toward her. He'd been trying to avoid this exact confrontation, but he couldn't any longer. "Janelle, I like you. You're a good friend, but that's it. I think you feel more for me than I feel for you." He saw the moment she began to understand because her eyes began to water. "I never meant to hurt you, but I thought you understood that we were just friends." *Shit, shit, shit.* This was not the place to do this, but he couldn't let it go on any more. It would only hurt worse later.

"I thought—" She wiped her eyes and took a deep breath. "It's my own fault." Her words said one thing, but the hurt look on her face told him quite another.

"I didn't mean to give you any indication that I was interested in anything beyond friendship, but if I did, I apologize." Len didn't know what else to say, and thankfully, Janelle didn't press him. She just nodded softly and left the barn without another word. A few minutes later, Len heard her car start and then pull away.

Len felt bad for her. It felt like this was his fault. Cliff had been right: he should have listened to him. He hoped she'd be able to get past this and they could return to being friends, but he wasn't so sure. Resigning himself to the loss, he picked up his tools and went back to work.

Randy returned for lunch, and they ate together. "You've been really quiet. I may as well be eating alone."

"Sorry, I'm just preoccupied today." He couldn't get Janelle off his mind. He'd hurt her, and even though it wasn't intentional, he wasn't happy about it, either.

Randy finished his lunch and put his things away. "If we get some rain, we should be able to cut hay in the next week or so. We'll need to find people to help. The hay needs to be cut and then left to dry for three days. Then it gets baled and loaded into the loft. It's quite a production."

"I helped load hay when I was a kid, but all I did was place the bales on the lift. I've never actually worked the rest of the process."

Randy smiled devilishly. "Since you did so good with planting, you can cut and turn the hay."

"I take it that is another of those jobs that requires hours in the tractor."

"How'd you guess?"

"You were too damn happy to have me do it." Randy hated sitting in the tractor. He'd rather be doing things with his hands than spend days driving around fields. "Come on, we need to get back to work. And just because I like you, I'll drive the tractor." Randy slapped him on the back, smiling at him before leaving the barn.

As the afternoon wore on, the heat and humidity continued to climb. Len had finished most of the heavy work earlier in the day, so he puttered around the barn, cleaning and making sure everything was organized before bringing in Thunder and Misty from their pastures and getting them ready for his ride with Cliff.

"I REALLY love this place." The creek babbled softly as they rested on the blanket in what had become their place. The slight breeze rustled the leaves, and Len was resting on his back with Cliff next to him. Up to now, Len had been the aggressor when it came to sex, hell, when it came to *anything* in this relationship with Cliff. But he was hoping that if he were patient, Cliff would take the lead.

"Me too. This clearing holds a lot of memories. I used to come here when I wanted to hide from Dad. Once, after I'd decided that his horse would look better blue and used Rit dye on him, I hid out here for hours until I thought he'd cooled down."

Len slid his hand along Cliff's leg. "Did it work?"

"Are you kidding? He tanned my hide but good. For a year, he brought everyone to see that horse just to show them what his crazy kid had done. I still have relatives who won't let me live that down."

Love Means ... *Courage*

"How old were you?"

Cliff got that look that told him something was coming. "I was twelve and really stupid." Len waited. "But I got to ride the horse in the Fourth of July parade, though."

That did it. Len cracked up. "You're kidding?"

"No, it was the only year the town had a blue horse. I rode with a white horse on one side and a red horse on the other. We were very patriotic." Len was about to laugh, but the urge left him as he felt a pair of lips against his neck. Arching his head back, he felt those lips travel toward his ear and then to his lips. Len returned the kiss ardently but kept his hands on the blanket.

"You taste so good," Cliff murmured. Len felt a hand slip beneath his T-shirt and slide up his belly, lightly stroking his skin. "I want you naked."

Len smiled against Cliff's lips. "Then get me naked." Cliff lifted his head, and Len saw the desire in those eyes. "Take what you want, anything you want, and make me yours." Cliff's lips crashed onto his, the kiss hard and possessive. This was what he'd hoped for—that given the chance, Cliff would stake a claim to him, tell him in his own way that Len was his.

Cliff lifted his lips away from Len's only long enough to pull off their shirts, and then the lips were back, taking what they wanted, and tongue devouring Len's mouth. Hands opened Len's pants, sliding down the zipper, pushing the denim past Len's hips. "I want you, Len, want you so bad."

"Then make love to me, Cliff." The lips stopped, and Len felt Cliff's entire body tense, Cliff's eyes locking onto Len's. *Damn it, I pushed too hard.* But the lips returned with more vigor, and Len shimmied his pants off his legs, lying naked beneath Cliff's firm body.

Cliff lifted himself up, standing and opening his pants, eyes gleaming as he looked at Len's prone body. "Are you sure this is what you want?"

Len met Cliff's gaze. "Only if you mean it, Cliff. I don't want you to do anything you don't want, or say anything you don't really mean." Len watched as Cliff's pants slid down his legs, pooling by his feet. Two quick steps later, Cliff was naked, his body pressing Len's against the soft earth. Their lips rejoined, and Len felt Cliff's ardor against his hip as hot skin slid against his. "I've waited for you to make love to me for a very long time," Len whimpered into Cliff's ear. "I had a huge crush on you in high school, but I've come to love you over the past couple months."

"You have? You do?" Len nodded against Cliff's lips as his skin was caressed. Lifting his legs, he wrapped them around Cliff's hips, offering himself to Cliff, letting him know that he was willing and eager to give him his most private, most intimate, self. Cliff's eyes shone with understanding and what Len read as love.

Cliff's hands slid along Len's thighs until fingertips brushed over his opening. The gentle touch sent a shock wave through him, and he shivered against Cliff's body, holding on tight as in case he only got to do this once. He'd told Cliff how he felt. Told him that he loved him, and while Cliff hadn't said it back, his hands and body were talking pretty loudly on their own. Cliff's head dipped slightly, and his tongue made little circles around a nipple, teasing the flesh ever so slightly. "Cliff, please." His knew he was whining, but he didn't care. "Please don't tease me."

"I don't have anything… won't it hurt you?" That tongue spun around his nipple again, this time with a little more force.

"Here." Len handed him a small tube of Vaseline he'd had in his pocket. "I need you, Cliff. Need to know what you feel like inside me."

Love Means ... *Courage*

"I've never done this." Cliff's voice was sweet, filled with concern and uncertainty.

"Use your fingers to start." Cliff nodded and a few seconds later, Len felt a long, thick digit slowly work its way inside him, making small circles as it slipped past the guardian muscle and deeper into his body. "Do you feel a small bump?" Cliff nodded. "Rub it slightly." Cliff nodded again, and a zing flashed along Len's spine.

"Are you okay?" Cliff began to remove his finger.

"Yes, more than okay. Do that again." Cliff complied, and Len felt his eyes roll to the back of his head.

"That's good, huh?"

"Yes, very good. You can try another finger." Cliff nodded and a second finger joined the first, stretching the muscle with a slight burn that quickly faded to pleasure as Cliff kept massaging that special spot. "Yes! Please, Cliff."

Then the fingers slipped from his body, replaced by Cliff, as he slowly and insistently pressed inside. "Cliff, so big." He felt Cliff breach his muscle and slide deeper into him. "So good." He moaned softly as Cliff filled him fully, resting against his hips, and started to pull back. Len put his hand on Cliff's hip to still him and give himself time to adjust. "Not yet." Cliff nodded, waited, and then slowly pulled back before filling him again.

"Yes!" With Len's encouragement, Cliff began aggressively thrusting, going deep and long until Len's cries filled the clearing. "Make me yours, Cliff, make me yours!"

Cliff drove into him. "You are mine and only mine."

Those were the words Len had longed to hear for a long time. They went from his ears directly to his heart, and his body reacted, spilling his passion onto his stomach in long white ribbons as Len felt the earth move beneath him, with Cliff following along right behind him, pouring himself deep into his lover.

Len fought through the haze of passion, looking into Cliff's eyes as a low rumble vibrated along the ground. "Did you hear that?"

Cliff nodded slowly. "I thought it was my heart pounding in my ears." The vibration repeated, followed by a low rumble, and Cliff smiled as he slipped from Len's body. "How's that for a seal of approval?" Len returned Cliff's smile and slowly lifted himself off the blanket and began getting dressed.

"Stay with me tonight."

Len stopped what he was doing, one leg in his pants. "Are you sure?"

The look in Cliff's eyes left no doubt. "Yes. I want to sleep with you, hold you, and love on you all night long."

Len nodded and grinned as he finished pulling on his pants, feeling his skin heat beneath Cliff's passionate gaze. Once dressed, they rolled up the blanket and mounted the horses again, riding back as fast as they could safely go. By the time they reached the barn, the sky was dark and ominous. Randy had already gotten most of the horses inside, and they got the last remaining ones into the barn as the first drops of life-giving rain began to fall.

CHAPTER 13

"YOU have a real knack with them, you know that?" Len turned to look at Cliff as he scratched Misty's nose. The two of them were alone in the barn. The afternoon storm had already passed. "They really seem to trust you," Cliff added.

"I think it's because I give them treats."

Cliff moved much closer. "I think it's because you have a good heart, and they can sense that."

Oh, he liked that. Liked having Cliff close to him, and he really liked the possessive, sexy leer on Cliff's face.

"Come on, Len—you have a kind, caring heart. Why do you think Geoffy loves you so much?" He stepped a little closer, and Len turned from the horse and looked him in the eye, waiting. "You're going to make me say it, aren't you?"

"Yes, Cliff. If you never say it again, I'll understand, but you have to say it once. I need to hear it. But only if you mean it."

Cliff stepped even closer, his feet almost touching Len's, heat from his body radiating across the space between them, close enough he could feel Cliff's breath against his face. "Yes, I mean it. That's why it's so hard to say, because once it's said I can't take it back." Cliff brought his lips so close to Len's he could feel their warmth. "I love you, Len Parker."

A sound in the yard broke the spell, and they reluctantly separated, each huffing slightly at the interruption, but neither of them was ready for their relationship to become public knowledge.

Len looked toward the door as Cliff whispered, "We need to talk about this, you know." Len turned back to Cliff and nodded as a group of kids that Len recognized as some of Nicole's students descended on the barn, laughing and giggling as they separated and started grooming their horses. Len wasn't surprised to see Nicole following right behind them.

She walked right up to Len, seeing the puzzled look on his face. "I didn't have time to cancel the lesson. The storm came up too quickly, but I figured they could spend some time grooming their horses and getting their tack ready for the fair next month."

"Ah. I figured the ring was too wet for them, but it should be all right by tomorrow." He led Nicole through the barn, taking a quick glance at Cliff as he did. "I fixed the drainage problem in the far section." He pointed across the ring. "You can see it looks good now. If it doesn't rain more tonight, you should be able to use it tomorrow with no problem."

"I'm not counting on it. They're calling for more storms tonight, and I've already canceled my lessons for tomorrow morning." Len nodded, and Nicole continued. "I got a call from Padgett saying he's in the process of rebuilding his barn. He said we could move our horses back in about a month."

"Oh." That was a huge blow to Len, who hadn't realized that the deal with Nicole was only temporary.

Love Means ... *Courage*

"I told him that we'd be staying right here. You keep this barn so clean, and the horses are wonderfully cared for, I couldn't ask for a better place." Len couldn't keep the smile off his face as she leaned close. "Besides, just between you and me, I've never liked old man Padgett. He's too closed-minded, if you know what I mean."

Len wasn't sure, but he was hoping he did. He really wanted to ask her what she meant, but one of her students pulled her away before he could ask. He turned and went back inside, meeting Cliff on his way.

"Mari was just about to leave. She asked me to say hi, and she told me that Geoff drove her crazy all day asking for you and wanting a 'hossey wide'." Len smiled at Cliff's imitation of his son. "Do you have time?"

Len chuckled. "Sure. I have time. I haven't unsaddled Misty from our ride."

God, the grin on Cliff's face was worth a mint. "I'll go get him. Thanks." Cliff looked around and saw all the people in the barn, leaned forward, and whispered. "I'll give you your thank-you later."

Len had to stop himself from quivering with anticipation and drooling as he watched Cliff's tight, jeans-encased butt move away.

"He's something isn't he?" He turned, looking square into Nicole's eyes. Shit, she'd seen him looking, and he didn't know what to say. Nicole just smiled at him and patted his shoulder as she yelled to all her students, "Meet me in the tack room in ten minutes."

"Geoff, slow down!" Len saw a small streak race through the barn door and down the aisle followed by a smiling and laughing Cliff. Damn, the smile he got shot right to his groin.

"Wen, hossey wide." Len squatted down and scooped Geoff into his arms to peals of laughter and little boy giggles.

"Yes. You can have a horsey ride."

"Yay!" Geoff did some sort of squirmy happy dance in Len's arms.

Len handed the wiggling boy to Cliff. "I need to go get Misty, and I'll lead you and Geoff around the yard. Do you have a camera? I'll take a picture of the two of you."

"I'll go get it and be right back." Cliff carried Geoff with him, and Len opened Misty's stall and walked her out of the barn and onto the lawn. Cliff met him, carrying both Geoff and the camera.

He put Geoff down and slipped the camera around Len's neck before mounting Misty and settling in the saddle. Len handed Geoff up to him and waited until he was settled before starting to lead Misty around the yard.

Geoff was having a ball, yelling, "Go, hossey, go," giggling, and smiling. After leading her toward the fence, Len stopped and handed Cliff the reins. Stepping back, he opened the camera and snapped a number of pictures of father and son together on the horse.

"Can you image him when he's a little older riding his first P-O-N-Y?"

Cliff grinned. "I had a P-O-N-Y when I was five. I got her for my birthday. Her name was Sugar, and she was the sweetest thing. I loved her to death. The first night I got her, I asked if I could sleep in the barn with her, 'cause 'She'd get lonely.'"

To Geoff's obvious dismay, Cliff lifted the youngster off Misty's back and handed him to Len. "You ride, and I'll lead you around for a while." Len mounted the horse, and Cliff handed up Geoff, who immediately settled down once he'd gotten what he wanted. Cliff snapped some pictures of them before taking a turn leading them around the yard.

"Hi, guys. Would you like me to get a picture of the three of you?"

Len turned and saw Mari coming out of the house. "I thought you'd left."

"I was just about to when I saw you giving rides."

Cliff turned to his sister. "Would you like a turn?"

"After I get pictures of the three of you." Cliff handed Len the reins and stood next to Misty, and Mari snapped a number of pictures. Then they all changed places, and Len led Mari and Geoff around the yard after the requisite pictures while Cliff went inside to start dinner.

As he led Mari and Geoff around the yard, a thought struck him. Cliff loved him, and Geoff loved him. Being gay, the one thing he never thought he'd have was a family of his own. Granted, it was really Ruby's family, but deep in his heart, he knew she wouldn't mind. In fact, she'd be pleased that her family was being taken care of by someone she cared about.

After a few last turns around the yard, Mari handed Geoff down and dismounted. "Thank you. I haven't been on a horse in a while."

"Why don't you ride? The horses need to be exercised, and if you let me know, I can have one ready for you."

"Do you ride much, Len?"

"Cliff and I go three or four times a week." He most certainly wasn't going to tell her where they rode or what they did, and he definitely wasn't going to invite her along.

"I know." Mari got this weird look in her eye. "You and Cliff both return from those rides happy and, ah… very relaxed." There was a wicked smirk on her face. Len had to tell himself that there was no way Mari could know what they were doing, that she was just being funny. But he still got a very unsettled feeling in his stomach. "I should get going." She walked to her car and quickly drove off as Len walked Misty back to her stall, unsaddled her, and got her ready for the night.

Once everything was set, he walked to the back door and knocked lightly. Cliff appeared almost immediately and opened it. "You don't need to knock; just come on in."

Len walked inside and closed the screen door after him. "I need to call Mom and let her know I won't be home."

"What are you going to tell her?" Cliff suddenly looked very concerned.

"The truth: that I'll be home tomorrow morning. She knows about me and how I feel about you."

"She does?" Cliff's surprised look was priceless.

"Yes, I told her a few years ago. She was super-supportive and understanding. Looking back on it, I don't know why I was so scared that she wouldn't understand. She has always been a great mom, and I wondered afterward if I thought she'd suddenly stop being a great mom because I was gay." *Fear makes you do stupid things.*

Cliff returned to his cooking. "I wish I'd had your courage."

"Things worked out for the best. You had Ruby, and you've got Geoff because of the choices you made. I'd say you made out pretty well."

"I guess I did." Len slipped his arms around Cliff's waist, pressing his chest to Cliff's back. "I really did."

Love Means ... *Courage*

The sound of toy car crashes and "broom, brooms" interrupted their romantic interlude, and Len nipped at Cliff's ear before releasing him and going to find Geoff in the living room.

Cars were strewn everywhere along with toy horses, trucks, blocks, and everything else he'd been playing with. "Didn't anyone ever tell you to put your toys back in the toy box when you were done?" Geoff just looked up at him with big eyes and shook his head. "Well, then, why don't we put the toys you aren't playing with in your toy box? That way, you'll be able to find them."

Len began picking up all the blocks, putting them in their bag and then putting it into the toy box. "I bet I can pick up more cars than you can." Len began racing around the living room, picking up cars and putting them in the box. Geoff followed Len's lead and began running around, his little legs and diapered butt just flying. "I'm gonna pick up more than you."

Scream and giggles floated through the room. "No you not! I'm beadin you." He continued zipping around on his little legs.

Len noticed Cliff standing in the doorway trying to keep himself from laughing as Len tricked Geoff into picking up and putting away his toys. "Dinner will be ready in about ten minutes."

Len smiled as the last of the cars disappeared into the toybox. "Let's get the horses into their stable." Len found a cloth bag that still held a few solemn horses, and he held it out as Geoff ran around picking up all the animals and putting them in the bag. They'd just finished when Cliff called them to dinner.

Geoff ran into the kitchen, and Cliff lifted him into his chair and placed his dinner on the tray before putting a heaping plate in front of Len. They'd just started eating when the phone rang. Cliff answered it and then handed the receiver to Len. "It's your mom." His voice had that fake "you're-in-trouble" tone.

"Hi, Mom."

"Are you coming home for dinner?"

"I'm sorry. I got busy here and forgot to call." He felt like a little kid. "I'll be home in the morning."

The line was quiet. "Oh." Was she angry? "Well, it's about time. I'll see you in the morning, then."

"Thanks, Mom. I love you."

"I love you too. Sleep well." He heard his mother laugh as she hung up the phone. Len handed the receiver back to Cliff, and he hung it up.

"Is everything okay?"

Len grinned back at him. "It's just fine."

Geoff began talking really fast and seemed to be trying to tell them all about his day, but they could only understand part of it. It didn't matter, though.

"We close on Mari's house next week." Cliff seemed so relieved and happy, with no sign of the grump bucket he'd been earlier in the day.

"That's great. So does that mean you'll be able to make it to harvest?"

"Yeah, and with the price of corn, we just might manage to have a good year."

"I'll second that." They raised their water glasses, and Geoff raised his sippy cup, and they toasted with smiles and laughter.

After dinner, Cliff took Geoff upstairs and gave him his bath before getting him ready for bed. Len sat in the living room and watched television, such as it was. With only two, sometimes three stations, there wasn't much variety.

Love Means ... *Courage*

"Len," Cliff called from the top of the stairs. "Geoff wants you to read him a story." With a smile, Len turned off the television and went upstairs, following Cliff to Geoff's bedroom.

He was already tucked in bed, hugging a stuffed mouse, eyes gleaming expectantly at Len. "What story would you like?" There was a crib still in one corner of the room leading Len to believe that Geoff had recently graduated to his big-boy bed.

"George."

Cliff handed him a well-loved copy of *Curious George*, and Len sat on the edge of the bed and began to read. By the time he finished the story, Geoff was asleep. Cliff kissed his son gently on the head before turning out the light and leading them out of the room and down the hall.

"I need to close up the house, but I'll be right back." Cliff opened the door to his bedroom and thumped down the stairs. Len went into the room and sat on the edge of the bed, waiting for Cliff. A few minutes later, he heard him climb the stairs again. Cliff appeared in the doorway looking sexy as hell, and then he was in Len's arms, kissing him hard and pressing him back onto the mattress.

LEN woke as thunder rumbled in the distance, a stiff breeze fluttering the bedroom curtains. As he watched, lightning flashed, and a louder rumble of thunder sounded—a deep roll that shook and vibrated the very earth itself. "You okay?"

"I'm fine. The thunder woke me up." Cliff made a deep throaty sound and then moved closer, their legs entwining as their lips found the others. Lightning flashed again, and then a sharper clap of thunder sounded in the distance.

"Daddy!" The door to the room, which Cliff had left cracked so he could hear Geoff, was pushed open. "Daddy?"

"Yes, Geoff." Tiny steps raced across the room, and then a small body climbed onto the bed. Both men quickly fished for their underwear, pulling them on under the covers as Geoff, still carrying his stuffed mouse, burrowed under the covers between them.

"Night, Daddy. I wuv you." Len heard Geoff kiss his dad on the cheek. Then Geoff rolled over. "Night, Wen. I wuv you." Then he felt Geoff kiss his cheek, and the small body rolled onto his side, hugging his mouse to him. Len smiled and stretched his arm up over Geoff's head, and he felt Cliff's hand slide into his.

CHAPTER 14

THE morning dawned crisp and clean, a cool breeze blowing through the open window, light just beginning to peek through. Len's internal clock went off at what had now become his usual time, and he got out of bed and headed to the bathroom. Once he was cleaned up, he padded back to his bedroom to get dressed and then headed to the kitchen, meeting his mother along the way.

"I see you came home yesterday." She squeezed his shoulder as she made her way to the kitchen.

"I've only stayed at Cliff's a few nights." He wanted to stay more often, but he wasn't willing to push, particularly since any relationship with Cliff involved a relationship with Geoff as well, and there was no way he was going to hurt that little boy if he could help it.

"I know. I'm glad you're happy, but I hope you're not rushing into anything." She started the coffee maker and leaned against the counter. "I just don't want you to get hurt. This can be a wonderful area, but it can also be mean, and if your relationship with Cliff gets out, there could be some hatred directed your way."

"I know, but we'll cross that bridge when we come to it." He inhaled deeply and let it out slowly. "Fred already knows, and I'm pretty sure Randy does as well." He also thought Cliff's sister Mari and Nicole Robinson might suspect that there was something going on between them, but neither had come right out and asked.

"I'm not saying everyone is going to hate you. There will be people who'll accept you and Cliff without question, but people can be violent when they hate." She poured two cups of coffee and handed one to Len. "You're still my son, and I'm just worried about you."

"I know you are." Len leaned down and kissed her on the cheek before walking back to his bedroom to finish getting ready for work. Sipping his coffee, he finished getting dressed and packed a bag for the afternoon. Cliff and Geoff had asked him to go to the beach that afternoon, and he was looking forward to it: warm sand, sun, Geoff playing, Cliff in a wet bathing suit. Now that was worth getting up early for.

When he had everything ready, he finished his coffee, grabbed his bag, and left his room, dropping his cup in the sink and saying goodbye to his mother before leaving the house. Starting the car, he turned on the radio as usual. "A fatal accident on US-10 left two dead and one injured. The police aren't releasing the names of the victims, pending notification of relatives." The announcer moved right on to another topic. "The drought in the plains continues to drive farm prices. According to The Andersons of Maumee, Ohio, corn closed up another five cents at two ninety-five a bushel, and beef futures closed up another four cents per pound." The announcer continued with the rest of the futures report, but Len already had the information he needed and turned off the radio, continuing his drive in silence.

Pulling into the farm, he parked and headed straight into the barn and got to work. He tried to get some stalls cleaned every day so it didn't get away from him, but with most of the horses spending their time in the pastures because of the weather, there were only a few stalls to clean, and he got those done right away.

"Hey, Len. You ready to cut some hay?" Randy strode up, looking gleefully happy, followed by Fred, who looked pleased with himself for some reason.

"Is that smile because you don't have to do it?"

"Yup. I'm mending fences today." Len would rather ride on a tractor than mend fences, so it was fine with him. They were both hot, dusty jobs anyway. "I've got the tractor all set up for you, and I can show you what you need to do when you're ready."

"Thanks." Len turned to Fred. "What's got you so happy?"

Randy elbowed Len in the ribs. "He's got a date with Susie Cooper tonight."

"Don't pick on him too much. He went pretty light on you when you started dating Shell, remember?" Randy looked sheepish, and they reviewed their tasks for the day. "This afternoon, I'll be away with Cliff for a few hours. We're taking Geoff to play at the beach."

Randy and Fred looked at each other and around them before looking back at Len. "Are the two of you getting serious?" Randy asked in a hushed tone.

"I think so, yeah." Randy nodded but didn't say any more. "Is there something you wanted to ask?"

"No. Other than to tell you that I have a cousin who's gay, and she's really great." Randy began to fidget, and Fred took over. "What we're saying is that we both understand, and that it's not a big deal. That's not to say it won't be with others." They trailed off, not sure what to say, and Len let them off the hook gracefully.

"Thank you. That means a lot." It really did. Len had expected a lot of problems—maybe not from Fred and Randy, because of what Fred had said before—but even Cliff's sister had been hinting and acted like it didn't bother her. He and Cliff definitely needed to talk about this.

Fred moved them along. "We need to get started."

Randy got the tractor out and showed Len how to operate the hay cutter, and then they were off. Len spent the next eight hours on the tractor mowing wide swaths of hay and leaving it to dry behind him. Unfortunately for Len, the tractor was not enclosed, so he sweated up a storm, having to wear a long-sleeved shirt and a hat to keep from getting sunburned. It was truly hot and dusty work. At four o'clock, he pulled the tractor into the equipment shed and turned off the engine.

"Is that Len, or is there a dust monster driving my tractor?" Cliff approached and jumped onto the one of the wheel covers, leaning down to give him a kiss. "How'd it go?"

"Okay. You seem happy."

"I am. Mari and I closed on her house today, the price of corn and beef are up, and it looks like we could have a very good year because of it." Cliff couldn't help looking at the sky. "As long as it doesn't rain until we get the hay in."

"First you want rain, then you don't. Could you make up your mind? I'm getting whiplash here." Len smiled, and Cliff kissed him.

"Are you ready to go?"

"I still have a few more fields to go, and I thought I could cut them when we got back."

"You could do it tomorrow." Cliff's hand on his thigh almost made him forget what he'd been thinking.

Love Means ... *Courage*

Len shook his head. "Tomorrow I have to turn what I cut today so we can bail everything and start bringing it in next week. I don't want to take any chances on rain spoiling the hay. It's supposed to rain the middle of next week, if the weather report is to be believed, and I want this hay in before it does." Len got up off the seat, and his legs buckled slightly beneath him.

"Get down carefully; you've been sitting a long time." Cliff helped him down, and he grabbed his things and put them in Cliff's truck. A few minutes later, he saw Cliff and Geoff come out of the house, with Geoff skipping excitedly behind his dad, carrying a beach pail and shovel. Geoff raced to the truck, and after Cliff lifted him in, he settled in his seat and waited to be buckled in, talking and jabbering the entire time.

"Is everybody ready?" Cliff called out.

A small chorus of yes's answered, and Cliff pulled out of the drive and sped off down the road toward the lake. "I thought we'd go the state park. The water will be warmer at Hamlin Lake than it will be in Lake Michigan."

"Sounds good. Is that okay with you, Geoffy?" Len tickled the boy's tummy, and he giggled loudly. Geoff pointed out the highlights as they drove, his young eyes fascinated by everything he saw. "Ows, Daddy. Hos, Wen. Piddys, piddys." Those little hands pointed out and named every farm animal they saw.

As they pulled into the state park, Cliff bought a sticker, and they headed toward the lake. Geoff could barely contain himself when they pulled into the parking lot and he saw all the people and kids gathered on the beach. Cliff carried all the things, and Len got Geoff out of his seat and carried him over the hot pavement and onto the beach. "Why is it that I have to carry everything?" Cliff groused teasingly as he dropped their things on the sand.

"Ask Geoff. It was his idea." Geoff had insisted that he wanted Len to carry him to the beach, which left Cliff to deal with all the stuff. Len set Geoff on the sand, and he immediately grabbed his bucket and shovel and began digging. "Go change, and I'll stay here with Geoff."

"Okay, I'll be right back, and then you can change." Cliff leaned close. "I'm looking forward to seeing that butt of yours in a bathing suit." *Thanks, Cliff.* There was no way Len could be seen in a bathing suit right now. Every time Cliff used that bedroom voice on him, Len got excited, fast.

Cliff walked to the changing room, and Len began slathering Geoff with sunscreen after pulling off his shirt. Cliff returned and scooped Geoff into his arms. "You want to go in the water with Daddy?" Geoff nodded and squealed as Cliff walked them both toward the water, and Len grabbed his suit and headed off to change.

Most of the buildings in Ludington State Park were built during the thirties and forties, and the changing room was no exception. One of the unique features was that the restrooms were vented to one another near the ceiling, so sound traveled from one restroom to the other. So while Len was in there changing, he could hear voices floating over from the ladies restroom. Normally, he wouldn't pay attention, but one voice stuck out from the rest—it sounded familiar. Len slipped into a stall and quickly changed his clothes.

He emerged from the bathroom, walking quickly back to where Cliff and Geoff were playing near the edge of the water.

"Wen, pway wif us."

Len knelt on the sand and began working on the monster sand castle they were building. "Janelle's here."

Cliff stopped working for a second. "So?"

"There are some things we need to talk about."

"Sounds pretty ominous."

"Don't mean it that way, but there are things we have to discuss."

Cliff looked up and smiled. "Okay." They walked to the blanket, from where they could keep an eye on Geoff. He seemed very occupied anyway, digging in the sand. "What's the problem?"

"There isn't a problem, per se. I just wanted you to know that our behavior is being noticed. Fred and Randy mentioned it today."

A flash of fear crossed Cliff's eyes. "What'd they say?"

"Nothing bad. They actually asked me if we were serious. They're cool with it, actually."

"They are?" It was like Cliff could barley believe his ears.

"Yes. They're good men who think the world of you and the farm."

Cliff shook his head slowly. "Well, I'll be damned."

"And I think your sister Mari might have an idea. She mentioned to me that we both seem to come back from our rides looking really happy. And Nicole Robinson even insinuated something."

Cliff's eyes clouded quickly, and Len knew what the look meant. "So what are you saying? That you don't want to be together anymore?" He hissed through his teeth in a menacing whisper.

"No. That's not what I'm saying at all. I just think we should decide how we want to handle it. I'm not ashamed of you, and I'm not ashamed of loving you. I won't lie when asked about us. I've lied enough about it in my life; I won't do it anymore."

That fiery look in Cliff's eyes faded just as quickly as it flared. "Oh." Len waited to see how Cliff was going to react. "I agree."

You could have knocked Len over with a feather. He'd been expecting more resistance. "You do?" That was almost too easy.

"Yeah, I'm not ashamed of you either. I won't be shouting it from the rooftops, but I won't deny it either."

"You know I'd kiss you right here, but that would probably be too much like shouting it from the rooftops." Len said with a slight smirk.

"Well, don't you look cozy?" They both looked up and saw Janelle along with a very pregnant Vikki approaching from across the parking lot.

Len noticed that Cliff ignored her tone. "Hi, you two. Came down here to cool off?" Vikki began opening the folding chair she was carrying. Len jumped to his feet and helped her get it settled on the sand before she slowly lowered herself into it.

"I've been sweating like a pig ever since I got pregnant, and this heat isn't helping one bit." Len reached into the small cooler they'd brought and handed her a cold soda. "Thank you." She rolled the can on her face before popping open the top.

"So is it normal for employers to bring their employees to the beach?"

God, what a bitch! Len was starting to wonder why he'd never noticed it before. There must have been signs he'd missed. "I told you last week that I'd promised Geoff that I'd go with him to the beach." As if on cue, Geoff ran up to them pointing at the water. "Wen, simmin." He took hold of Len's hand and began dragging him toward the water. "Simmin. Wen, simmin."

Cliff took hold of Geoff's other hand to get his attention. "Do you need to go potty?"

"No, Daddy." The look on Geoff's face was priceless. "Simmin." Len got up and scooped Geoff into his arms as he walked into the cool water. Some kids splashed them, and Geoff slapped the water trying to splash them back. Len lowered them so just their head stuck out of the water and then jumped up. Geoff laughed and squealed as he did it again. Their play time was cut short when Geoff the said magic word. "Potty."

Len raced out of the water and walked up to Cliff, handing him his son, and the two of them took off for the bathrooms. "So Len, are you having fun playing house?"

"Excuse me?" Her attitude was starting to bother him. "There's no need to be mean, Janelle. I thought we were friends. I'm sorry you were hurt, but I never led you on."

Vikki looked up from her chair. "Jesus, Janie. I told you months ago he was just your friend. He never even kissed you, for God's sake. That should have been your first clue. There's no use getting yourself all upset anyway. Besides, I told you that Dan's cousin wanted to meet you." Vikki continued drinking her soda, fanning herself with a book. "Christ, it's hot." Vikki wedged herself out of the chair. "Take me home, Janie." She folded up her chair and began waddling back to the car.

Len stood on the sand and watched Janelle follow her. Never in his life was he so happy to see someone go. As they were leaving, he saw Cliff and Geoff came out of the bathroom, with Geoffy skipping along behind and smiling. Cliff saw his sisters and waved. They waved back and drove off.

"I see they left."

"Yeah. I think Janelle may be suspicious. She asked if I like playing house." Cliff settled on the sand next to him, and Geoff picked up his toys and continued playing.

"Don't worry about her. She can be a real pain in the a—" Cliff stopped himself just in time. "You know, but she's my sister and wouldn't deliberately hurt me. I think she felt more for you than she was willing to admit, and she's a little hurt."

Cliff looked to where Geoff was playing. They both joined him, playing together until Geoff stifled a yawn. "We're going to go in ten minutes, Geoff."

He didn't even look up. "Okay, Daddy."

"She'll get over it. Just give her time." Cliff said, alluding to their earlier conversation.

Len hoped Cliff was right, but he couldn't help wondering how Janelle would react when she found out that the man she was interested in was in love with her brother. Jesus Christ, his life was becoming a soap opera.

"Geoff, it's time to go."

Cliff wrapped a towel around his son and got him changed, and they walked back to the truck, carrying all the gear. "We can change back at the farm, if that's okay." Len agreed, and they loaded their things and pulled out of the parking lot. "How much more cutting is there to do?"

"About two hours."

"When you're done, come back to the house, and after dinner we can get cleaned up." The leer on Cliff's face left no doubt as to what he was thinking, and Len had to shift to keep his excitement from showing through his clingy, wet bathing suit.

Len swallowed. "Okay."

"Daddy, is Wen staying for dinner?"

"Yes, but he has work to do, and you'll be in bed before he's done."

Love Means ... *Courage*

"But I want him to wead George." Geoff was definitely tired. He rarely whined like he was doing now.

"If you're still awake when I'm done, I'll come in and read George for you. If not, I'll read it to you tomorrow. Okay?"

Geoff seemed mollified and rested his head against the side of his car seat, falling asleep before they were halfway home.

Pulling into the drive, Cliff took Geoff in the house, and Len went into the tack room, changed his clothes, and got the tractor started. It indeed took him another two hours to finish the cutting, and when he got back, he saw Cliff waiting for him by the back door with a tall, cold bottle. "I thought you could use a beer."

"Thanks." Len opened it and took a long slow gulp from the longneck.

"Geoff's asleep, and I have dinner ready. And afterward, I have something special planned. I already called Lorna and told her where you were. She laughed and told us to have fun."

"She really likes you, Cliff." Len hoped she did, because he was way past liking him.

"I think so," Cliff said. Len finished his beer and put the bottle in the trash. "Come on inside. Let's get you fed and loved."

"I like the sound of that." He leaned close and felt Cliff's lips on his.

CHAPTER 15

DINNER was quiet, just the two of them. The house was dark, the only light coming from the lamp above the table.

"That was really good," Len said.

"It was just spaghetti and garlic bread. Nothing fancy."

"Food doesn't have to be fancy to be good. It's just like men."

"I have something for dessert, but I think we can have it later." Cliff leaned close, brushing his lips faintly over Len's. "I think we need to get you cleaned up and those muscles soothed out, or it'll hurt to walk tomorrow." Cliff pushed his chair back and brought his dishes to the sink before taking care of Len's. "Go on upstairs and get a shower. I'll finish up here and meet you."

Too full and tired to argue, Len pushed back his chair and quietly walked up the stairs, down the hall, and to the bathroom near Cliff's bedroom. Turning on the light, he stepped inside and closed the door. Taking a deep breath, he slowly removed his shirt, surprised at how sore his arms and shoulders were. Who'd have thought driving a tractor would do that? But he was definitely feeling it. Folding his shirt and setting it on the counter, he opened his pants and slipped them and his boxers down his legs. Every muscle screamed as he bent to remove his shoes before stepping out of his pants.

Straightening himself back up, he turned on the water to let it heat before stepping under the spray. The water felt so good, washing over his skin and loosening his aching muscles. A soft sigh escaped as he put his hands on the tile and let the water run over him.

The shower curtain moved forward, and Len felt a pair of hands slink around his waist as he was tugged upright against hard, hot skin. "Hey," Cliff said as his hands glided along Len's chest and neck before sliding across his stomach.

"Hey, yourself." A low rumble echoed from Len's chest as lips suckled at the base of his neck.

"I think we need to get you cleaned up." Cliff began lathering his hands before slowly and tantalizingly smoothing away the dirt and grime with handfuls of soap and slicked, mischievous fingers. Len let Cliff have his way. He was too tired and achy to protest or even return the favor.

"If you keep that up, it'll be all over," Len said as Cliff paid attention to the only muscle on his body that wasn't aching, at least not from work.

"None of that until I get you in bed," Cliff said. "So just relax and let me take care of you."

He must have squatted down, because Len felt hands slide over his legs and along his inner thighs. Then his butt was washed and fingers slid along his crease. Without thinking, he pushed back into the sensation, and Cliff slid his fingers over Len's entrance, gliding around the puckered skin. "Cliff. God."

"Just relax." The hands worked their way north, sliding over his back and kneading the muscles of his shoulders. "I need to wash your hair." Len nodded and soon fingers were rubbing shampoo through his hair and massaging his scalp, making the skin tingle. "Rinse yourself off." Len stepped forward, and the water again cascaded over him, washing away all the soap. "Dry yourself off and go lie on the bed. I'll be right there."

Len nodded and stepped out of the tub. Drying himself off, he wrapped the towel around his waist and walked into Cliff's bedroom, lying on his stomach on the bed. *God, this feels good.* The quilt had been pulled back, and the sheets felt wonderful on his skin. The breeze through the window blew over him. If Cliff didn't get there soon, he was going to fall asleep.

The bed dipped slightly, and Len felt a tug on the towel, and then it was gone. Hands roamed over his back, and he felt a weight on his legs. The tight muscles of his back began to relax as Cliff's hands worked those muscles deep and hard. "Scoot up and rest your head on the pillow." Len complied thoughtlessly, his mind already shutting down.

Lips joined those hands, kissing him softly as they followed the hands, kissing where he'd been touched. Over his shoulders, the back of his neck, down his back, a slight nip on his butt—each and all were stroked and kissed. "Roll over." Len did as the now-disembodied voice asked him. The lights were off, and his eyes had drifted closed a while ago. Then those hands and lips started again; his throat, arms, and hands, all were lovingly caressed and kissed. Chest and nipples sampled and smoothed. His stomach and hips loved and rubbed.

Len was nearly asleep when his eyes flew open as he was engulfed in a tunnel of warm wetness. "Cliff."

"Just relax and give it all to me." Then the words stopped as he was taken deep once again.

"I love your mouth." His breathing became shallow and irregular as he put his hands on Cliff's head and drove into him. Sleep was now the last thing on his mind. "Yes!" He could feel the pressure building deep, and he removed his hands and did his best to signal, but Cliff was like a man possessed, and with each signal, he just increased what he was doing, driving Len over the edge until he spilled himself deep and hard.

"Cliff!" He tried not to call out too loudly, but he couldn't help himself. Thank goodness the door was closed. Then his entire body flopped back on the bed, completely wrung out. He felt Cliff crawling up his body, planting kisses as he went, until their lips met.

Now that he was wide awake, there was no way he was letting Cliff get away now. Wrapping his arms around him, he pulled him down on top of him. "I thought you were going to fall asleep on me."

"You woke me up." Len ran his hands along Cliff's back. "What do you want?"

"You, always you." Cliff shifted on the bed, lifting Len's legs and pressing them to his chest.

"What are you doing?" A hot wet tongue slid along his crease. "Cliff ..." The tongue zeroed in on his opening, swirling at the skin, and Len made unintelligible noises. He thought he must sound like some wanton slut, but he really didn't care. Cliff was doing things to him he never imagined, and the last thing he wanted him to do was stop. Cliff had promised that he was going to get loved on, and he wasn't kidding.

The tongue slid away, and the bed shook. Then he felt Cliff press into him, and his body opened to him and drew Cliff in, filling him up, stretching and burning until the pleasure washed everything away but Cliff and him.

"I'm going to give you the loving of your life, so hold on." Cliff drew back and slowly pushed back in with agonizing slowness, dragging himself over the spot that Len knew drove him crazy. Each thrust, each movement, exaggerated Len's need.

"Cliff, please." Len fisted the sheets as his pleas went unanswered, and he was driven to passionate heights. Cliff leaned forward and kissed him hard, but still his pace remained unaltered.

"I'm going to love on you the way you deserve to be loved."

"Whether I can take it or not?" Len's eyes were clouding as they locked onto Cliff's, watching every movement, every gesture, every flex of his muscles.

"Oh, you can take it." He pulled out and slid back inside. "You love it." Finally, to Len's relief, he felt Cliff's pace quicken slightly, and he clamped down on him, tightening his muscles. He felt Cliff quiver and shake, so he did it again and again until Cliff's control broke and he began driving deep inside.

"Yeah, Cliff, give it to me." Len's encouragement had the desired effect, and true to his word, Cliff gave him the ride of his life. "So close."

"Me too, but not till I tell you." Cliff's control was becoming ragged. "Now, Len." With a few strokes of his hand, Len was coming, and he felt Cliff throbbing deep inside him.

With heaving breaths, Cliff withdrew, sprawling onto the bed next to Len, pulling him close. "You were terrific."

"So were you." Their lips found each other, and they kissed gently, sweetly, as hands softly caressed hot skin.

Completely sated and spent, Len yawned and his eyes fell shut. The bed bounced a little, and he heard footsteps recede and then return. A warm cloth soothed over his skin, and then Cliff was back holding him close. "Sleep, Love." Len was so tired, he barely heard what Cliff said, but even through the depths of his sleepy brain, he smiled slightly, and that was the last thing he remembered as sleep overtook him.

WHAT the hell is that noise? Len woke to the light streaming through the windows, but he knew that wasn't what had awakened him. Lifting his head, he saw Cliff still asleep next to him. Glancing at the clock, he saw he still had time to sleep. Then the sound of a door closing downstairs brought him fully awake. "Cliff, there's someone in the house."

"Huh, what?" The body next to him stirred and pulled him closer before beginning to snore softly again.

"Cliff, I heard a door closing downstairs. There's someone else in the house." Footsteps on the stairs brought Cliff upright as he began to get out of bed and look around the room.

"Cliff, are you up yet?"

"Shit, it's Janelle. What in the hell is she doing here at this time of the morning?"

Before either of them could get out of bed, the door opened and Janelle strode into the bedroom. "Cliff, I need to talk to you about this house you sold—" The words died on her lips as she looked at the bed and saw Cliff and Len lying together, both obviously naked. "What in the hell is going on?"

Cliff pulled the covers up over Len and sat up in bed. "What does it look like, Janelle? We're trying to sleep, for Christ's sake, and what in hell are you even doing here?"

"I knew you got up early, and I wanted to ask you about this house you sold to Mari." She couldn't take her eyes off Len lying in the bed next to Cliff. "But that can wait." She glared at Len. "What are you doing in Cliff's bed?"

Len looked at Cliff and then back at Janelle. "I'm sleeping with the man I love."

The wail she let loose sounded more like an animal that any noise ever uttered by a human being. "What?"

Len and Cliff heard, "Daddy?" and then the sound of crying followed by a rather panicked, "Daddy!"

Cliff threw back the covers on his side the bed and pulled on a pair of boxers. "Get your ass downstairs, Janelle. I will not have this conversation with you in my bedroom."

She crossed her arms over her chest. "I'm not going anywhere."

Cliff turned around. "Len, would you please get dressed and then call the police. Tell them there's an intruder in the house."

"You can't do that to me in my own home." Her voice had a plaintive tone.

Cliff wasn't giving an inch. "This is not your home, Janelle. This is *my* home."

"I grew up here."

"This… is… my… home! Now get your fat ass downstairs, or we will call the police and have you arrested!" He pointed toward the stairs and waited for her to move. When she hesitated, he added. "Don't make me shove you down them, because right now, I'd do it for a penny."

Len didn't know if it was Cliff's threat, the tone of his voice, or maybe it was the fire in his eye that got to her, but she spun around and walked down the stairs.

Cliff turned to Len, anger still blazing in his eyes. "I'm sorry."

"It's not your fault." Geoff was still crying, and they heard his cries getting louder. "Go see to Geoff, and I'll get dressed and meet you downstairs."

Cliff shook his head. "She's mine to deal with, not yours."

"We'll both deal with her. I'm not going to slink away and let you take all the heat. Remember, she's upset because you got me and she didn't."

Geoff appeared in the doorway, and Len pulled on his pants while Cliff picked up and comforted his son. "I'm sorry. Daddy and Aunt Janelle were having a fight."

"Say you sowwy." Everything was so simple to a two-year-old.

"Len is going to put you back in bed, and he'll read you George, okay?" Geoff put his head on Cliff's shoulder and nodded as he walked out of the bedroom. Len followed, and as Cliff settled Geoff back in his bed, Len sat in the chair and picked up the book. Geoff wasn't going to last long, but he opened it and started reading. Cliff leaned down and kissed him gently on the neck before straightening up. "Come downstairs when you're ready." Len nodded and began to read.

Geoff was asleep before he'd finished half the book. Len closed the pages and set the book aside. Getting out of the chair, he closed the door most of the way and went back into the bedroom. Finding his shirt from the day before, he put it on and headed downstairs.

In the living room, Cliff and Janelle were staring at each other, neither of them saying a word. When Len walked in, Janelle stood up and looked like she was going to start yelling again, but Cliff cut her off. "If you raise your voice and wake Geoff again, so help me God, I'll bodily throw you out of this house."

He stepped closer to her. "And don't think for one minute that I won't. Do you understand?" She nodded stiffly. "Good. Now why don't you tell me why you came here in the first place?"

"I wanted to know why you sold that house to Mari and not to me." She pulled a tissue out of her purse.

Cliff's anger hadn't abated much, and he was definitely in no mood for her theatrics. "First off, she told me she was interested, and we reached a deal. She paid market price for it, and I hold the land contract. That's all there is to it."

"But I might have wanted it too. You never asked either Vikki or myself."

Len watched as Cliff took a deep breath. "It never occurred to me. She asked, and we reached a deal. That's all there is to it. Now, I don't think you want to explore that subject any further." Len was surprised at the way Cliff cut off the talk, but he figured he had a reason. "As for the other subject for this morning, I will tell you this once and once only. I love Len and he loves me. He's my lover and the best friend I've ever had. We've been together for about a month now, and we're exploring a lasting relationship. This has nothing to do with you. Len told you that the two of you were just friends. Did he not?"

"Well yes. But…."

"At any time, did he kiss you?" She shook her head. "Hold your hand?" She shook her head again. "Touch you, or tell you in any way that he was interested in anything other than friendship?"

"No… but—"

"What, Janelle? Is it that I'm gay?" Len had to marvel at the way Cliff was keeping command of this conversation, keeping her on the defensive and framing the questions to keep her on the defensive rather than answering her questions. They both noticed that she didn't answer the last question. "That's it, isn't it?"

"How am I supposed to feel? I liked him, and I find out that he's gay and in love with my brother."

Len spoke for the first time. "We can't answer that, but you have to understand, I never meant to hurt you. And I tried to spare your feelings. I'm very sorry you feel hurt, but we were never going to be more than friends." She sniffled and dabbed her eyes with a handkerchief.

"There's one more thing we need to get straight. This is my home. You grew up here, as did Mari and Vikki, but if you barge in again like you did this morning, I'll have the locks changed. Now I suggest you leave. If you have questions or things you wish to discuss with us, we'll be glad to do that, but we expect you to call first."

Len checked his watch. "I'd also like to ask that you let me tell Vikki and Mari. This isn't something they should hear from you." They could almost see the wheels turning in Janelle's head. "If you wish to be mean, you could, but they'd both ask me about it, and I'd be forced to tell them how you found out. You wouldn't hold their sympathy for very long, and you know it."

"Okay, that seems only right."

"I'll tell them this afternoon. Now I think it's time you left. We have work to do. I'll call you this afternoon and let you know what's going on." Without another word, she got to her feet, her back ramrod straight, and left the house. She didn't say another word or look back as the door closed behind her.

Cliff sighed. "I'll make coffee. We're going to need it. I have a feeling this is going to be one hell of a day."

CHAPTER 16

LEN drove home to get some clean clothes. "Shit." He swerved to miss a squirrel and got back on the road. "Pay attention to your driving." His mind was definitely elsewhere. Janelle had walked in on him and Cliff together in Cliff's bed. He almost smiled, and it would actually have been funny if she weren't so scary right now. He pulled into the yard and parked next to his mother's car. Turning off the engine, he rested his head against the steering wheel.

Opening the door, he got out and went inside. His mother came out of her room and closed the door behind her. "I wasn't expecting to see you this morning."

"I need to get some fresh clothes." Len noticed that there was something different about his mother. She was smiling and seemed sort of graceful. Len peeked down the hall, looking at her closed bedroom door. Turning back to her, he smiled, and she blushed beet red. "Mom, are you seeing someone?" She blushed deeper and nodded her head slowly. "That's great. Does he make you happy and treat you right?"

Love Means ... *Courage*

She lowered her voice. "Yes, he does. He's one of the administrators at the hospital, and we've been seeing each other for a few weeks."

He mimicked her tone. "Why didn't you tell me?"

"I was waiting until I knew it was serious."

"Is it serious?" She nodded, and Len smiled, pulling her into a hug. "I'm very happy for you."

"Speaking of happy, how was your evening?"

"The evening was great. The morning was a little weird. Janelle walked in on us this morning, and you probably heard the fireworks from here."

"Were you... busy... at the time?" He could tell she was trying to suppress a smile.

"No, we were asleep when she barged into Cliff's bedroom."

His mother couldn't hold it in any more and burst into peals of laughter. "She was always too nosy for her own good. Serves her right." She started cackling.

"She let out a wail that sounded like a moose in heat."

Lorna completely lost it, cackling and laughing until her sides hurt. Eventually, her door opened, and a man Len didn't know stepped out and closed the door. "Are you all right, Lorna?"

"I'm fine." She managed to get a hold of herself. "Jerry, this is my son, Leonard. Len, this is Jerry Foster."

"It's nice to meet you. Lorna has told me a lot about you." He extended his hand, and Len shook it.

"I don't want to interrupt anything. I just need to get changed for work. I'll only be a few minutes." Len excused himself and went into his room, closing the door behind him. He changed quickly and packed a small bag to keep in the trunk of his car. When he was done, he opened the door and quietly walked to the kitchen.

Lorna seemed to be waiting for him. "You're really okay with Jerry and me?"

He pulled her into a hug. "Of course I am. You deserve someone who'll make you happy, and he seems really nice. So go back to him, and I'll see you later." He kissed her on the cheek and left the house, the drama with Janelle and Cliff's family temporarily forgotten as he drove back to work.

When he pulled into the drive at the barn, Cliff was waiting for him, looking very nervous. "My sisters will be here for lunch, and I'll tell them then."

"Cliff, there's nothing to be nervous about. These are your sisters, your family, and they love you. Besides, I think Mari already suspects."

"Should I tell the guys?" Cliff's mind was wandering.

"They already know, remember?" Len began leading him back toward the house. "Cliff, just relax. We've done nothing wrong."

"I know. I'm just worried that they'll hate me."

"They won't hate you. They may not accept it, but they won't hate you. No matter what, you're still their brother. Besides, if they're going to hate anyone, it'll be me."

"You? How do you figure that?"

"They'll hate me for corrupting their brother." Cliff glared at him. "I can just hear Janelle." Len mimicked her voice. "He wasn't gay until he met you."

"That's nonsense. I've had these feelings for as long as I can remember. I just denied them for most of my life."

Len opened the door and guided Cliff inside. "I know, and you need to help them understand that. But Cliff, I don't want to come between you and your family." It would break his heart if Cliff lost his family because of him, and he couldn't let that happen.

"What are you saying? That if they don't accept us, you'll leave?" Cliff turned to face him, his eyes blazing. "Is that it? You'll be magnanimous and leave to appease my family and what? Make me completely miserable? Leave me alone?" Cliff poked his finger in Len's chest. "Don't you fucking dare!" The heat in Cliff's eyes continued to blaze.

"Okay! We'll face this together, no leaving and no running. But it's not going to be easy. I hope you know that."

"Nothing worthwhile is."

"Don't be flip. This is important. Do you know what it means? There'll be people who won't want to do business with you anymore. You may have trouble finding help when you need it. This is a big step. I'm not saying you shouldn't do this; I'm just saying you need to do it with your eyes open."

"I am. My eyes are wide open." His expression softened. "For the first time, I know what it is I really want, and that's you with me. The rest of the world be damned. Besides, I'm not the one who'll have to deal with finding help when we need it. You will."

"I will?"

Cliff's eyes twinkled with delight. "Yes. As the new farm foreman, it's your responsibility. You've already told me that if I dealt with the hands, I'd run them off, so you're the foreman. Not that it's a big change. You've been doing the job almost since you arrived. I'm just making it official."

"But what about Fred and Randy? They've been here longer than I have."

"I already talked to them, and when I told them I was looking to hire a foreman to help run the farm, they both mentioned you. But there is one thing you need to do that you aren't doing now." That twinkle was back in Cliff's eye. "You need to organize a poker game for Friday nights. It seems you've been lax in that area." Cliff kissed him as they heard Geoff calling from upstairs. "Seems he's awake and our reprieve is over."

"I should get started anyway." Len took another kiss and then headed outside while Cliff climbed the stairs to get Geoff.

"I'll see you in time for lunch, and don't spend too much time on the tractor today." He disappeared upstairs before Len could say anything in response.

Leaving the kitchen, the screen door banged closed behind him. Len strode across the yard to the barn to get his work day started. After making sure all the horses had water and hay, he began the daily ritual of cleaning stalls.

The slamming of car doors announced the arrival of Fred and Randy, and they met in their usual spot and talked about what needed to get done.

Randy reluctantly agreed to split the tractor duties with Len, and everyone got to work, with Len taking the morning and Randy getting tractor duty in the afternoon. Then everyone got to work.

LEN drove the tractor back to the farm, parked in the drive before shutting it off, and headed right into the house. Cliff was already pacing, wandering from room to room, and stepping over Geoff's toys.

"Cliff, it's not the end of the world."

Love Means ... *Courage*

"I know. I'm just nerved up." Even his voice sounded nervous.

"Keeping busy will help with the nerves. Go make lunch, and Geoff and I will pick things up in here."

Len started the cleanup games with Geoff, and soon he was running around, picking up his things, with Len chasing him around the room. Once the toys were picked up, Len gave Geoff a few he could play with, and the toddler began running the trucks over the furniture.

Len went onto the kitchen to make sure Cliff was doing okay. "You need any help?"

"I'm almost done." Len could tell he was still nervous.

Slipping his arms around his lover's waist, Len planted a kiss near the base of his neck. "Just be honest with them and remember that what you're doing takes courage." The sound of closing car doors drifted in through the open windows. "Remember they're your family and they love you." Len let his hands slip away. "And try not to get frustrated." Len backed away. "Oh—" He replaced his hands. "Remember that I love you, no matter what." Len backed away just as the back door opened. Dan and Vikki came in, and Dan helped her into a chair.

"Would you like something to drink?"

"God, yes." Cliff got a tall glass of iced tea and set it on the table in front of her. "Thank you." She gulped from the glass. "Thank God I've got just a few more weeks." She held the glass to her forehead. Dan took a chair next to her and Cliff put a glass in front of him as well.

"Aun' Ikki." Geoff raced into the kitchen, and she bent down slowly and gave him a gentle hug. "You fat."

To her credit she smiled. "I'm going to have a baby."

His little eyes got wide as he stared at her tummy. "Like me?"

"Yes, but not quite as big."

He turned his head from side to side, his little mind puzzling. "How do you get it out?" All the adults began to laugh, and Vikki gave him a hug and sighed with relief when Cliff put Geoff in his chair and gave him his lunch.

The back screen door closed, and Mari walked in carrying a dish of salad, setting it on the table before giving her siblings hugs and settling in a chair. "How are you feeling, Vikki?"

"Like a balloon ready to pop."

Her husband's hand slipped into hers. "She's only got a few weeks, and we're trying to keep her as comfortable as possible." He rubbed her belly like a proud papa, and Vikki smiled back at him. Cliff brought her a glass of tea as well and started getting lunch on the table.

Mari got up to help. "So what is it you wanted to talk to us about?"

Cliff took a deep breath and sat at the table between Mari and Vikki. "I'm expecting Janelle, but she seems to be running late."

Just then a car pulled in, and a few moments later, Janelle walked into the kitchen, a sour look on her face.

"I asked you here because I have something to tell you." Len leaned against the counter on the other side of the kitchen, not wanting to intrude on the family gathering, but Cliff motioned for him to join them. "I don't know how to say this, so I'm just going to come out with it."

Janelle's voice cut him off. "You're going to tell them in front of Geoff?"

"Of course." Len turned specifically to watch Mari and Vikki. "I'm gay and I'm going to build a life with Len." Cliff turned to look at him. "If he'll have me." Now that the words were out and couldn't be taken back, Len could see Cliff visibly relax. Now the ball was in their court.

Both of them remained silent until Mari got to her feet and put her arms around Cliff's neck, giving him a hug. "Good for you."

Len saw Vikki turn to Dan, who just shrugged like it was no big deal, before she turned back to her brother. "What about Ruby? Did you love her?"

"Yes, I did. Very much. But I've always felt attracted to men, though I suppressed it for a long time. Len helped give me the courage to face who I really am." Cliff's words seemed to flow. Len glanced at Janelle, noticing the surprised look on her face, but to her credit, she kept her feelings to herself.

"So is Len going to live here with you?" Mari asked excitedly.

"We haven't discussed it yet."

Vikki motioned for Cliff to move closer to her. "Do you love him? And does he make you happy?"

Cliff looked at Len as he answered. "Yes I do. I love him very much, and he makes me very happy."

Vikki sat back and began to remove the covers from the food. "Can we eat now? I'm starved. This eating for two thing is absolutely true." Mari got up and helped Cliff get the lunch on the table.

"Is that it?" Janelle stood up. "Is that all you're going to say?"

Mari put the plates on the table. "What more is there to say?"

"How about that it's immoral and a sin? Or that it's wrong?"

Mari sat down and began passing the food. "Can it, Janelle. You were always so high and mighty, but you don't know crap, so get over it."

Vikki began filling her plate. "You can't fight the wind, Janie. Besides, if they love each other, that's all that matters. And when did you get so religious anyway?" Janelle just glared at them. "You can't do anything about it, so you just need to accept it and move on."

Len could hardly believe his ears. He'd expected Mari to be supportive, but it didn't seem to be a big deal to Vikki either.

Janelle stood glaring at them before picking up her purse. "We'll just see if I can't do something about it." Then the back screen door slammed, and they heard her car start up and drive off.

Mari patted his brother's hand. "She'll be fine. You just need to give her time." Len wasn't so sure, but he took the empty seat between Mari and Cliff.

Vikki scoffed. "Oh, please." She rolled her eyes and swished her fork as she spoke. "When have you ever known Janelle to change her mind about anything? The woman's as stubborn as a mule."

"So what happened to bring on this revelation? It was obvious from her question about Geoff that Janelle already knew."

Len took some salad and stared down at his plate. This one was all Cliff's.

"She came by the house early this morning to ask why I sold you the Henderson house, because apparently she wanted it. Anyway, she walked into my bedroom and—" Cliff didn't get to finish the sentence before Mari, Vikki, and Dan all started laughing. Geoff even got into the act, laughing and spraying food on his tray.

Love Means ... *Courage*

"That's one morning wake-up call neither of us is likely to forget any time soon."

CHAPTER 17

"HAVE you heard anything from Janelle?" Len was shoveling out the soiled bedding from Thunder's stall, peeking up at Cliff as he lifted Geoff so he could see what "Wen" was doing.

"Not a word, and that's so unlike her. We've had our disagreements over the years, and a few knock-down, drag-out fights, but usually when it's over, we talk it through and go on. She's such a talker, that to tell you the truth, I'm a little worried." Cliff settled Geoff on his shoulders so he could watch.

"She'll be fine, given time."

"It's been two weeks. It's not her hurt feelings I'm worried about. She can be as vindictive as hell when she wants to be, and the longer she's quiet, the more I wonder what she's going to pull." Len could hear the concern ringing in Cliff's voice.

"Maybe I should try to talk to her." Len finished loading the bedding wheelbarrow and wheeled it to the muck pile, with Cliff and Geoff walking along. When they got close to the pile, Geoff immediately held his nose.

Love Means ... *Courage*

"Stinky, Daddy."

"Yes, it is." Cliff returned to the conversation as they headed back inside. "Why would you do that?"

Len leaned on his shovel. "Cliff, she's hurting. In her mind, the man she thought of as her boyfriend—whether I was or not, is immaterial to her—is now involved with her brother. That's got to be painful for her." Len sighed loudly. "Though I don't know what to say to her, and I wish she hadn't found out about us the way she did."

"That was her own fault for being too pushy."

"I know, but it doesn't change the way she feels." Len picked up the shovel and got to work, the metal scraping on the concrete floor as he scooped. "Maybe Mari can help."

"Maybe. I'll call and see if she can convince Janelle to talk to us, or at least talk to Mari."

"Good." Len finished mucking out the stall and emptied the wheelbarrow, returning to the stall with a load of bedding. He decided to change the subject. "The first cutting of hay was very successful. The loft is three-quarters full, and with the additional horses, plus those additional bales we sold, we'll have used up the hay from last year in the next month. The second cutting should fill the loft and give us some additional to sell. If we get a third cutting, and it looks like we should, we'll bale it for the cattle."

"We'll need it. With the additional calves, the herd's growing nicely. And next year, I'm hoping to enlarge it even further. We have the land to support the larger herd now."

"When you're doing your projections, you might want to project an additional hand while you're at it." Len finished up the stall and put his tools away. "Tomorrow night's the fireworks at the high school. I was wondering if you and Geoff would like to go.

Mom's going with Jerry, and she asked if we'd like to go too. To tell the truth, I'm rather curious about Jerry."

"Sounds like fun." Cliff began tickling Geoff. "You wanna see the fireworks tomorrow, maybe get ice cream?" Geoff giggled and laughed as he tried to nod his head. "I'm declaring today an unofficial farm holiday. Tell the guys to get done and go home. They can start the holiday early." Cliff put Geoff in his sandbox, and he started playing, ignoring them as they talked. "And I thought we'd go into town tonight and have dinner. And afterward, maybe we'll make some fireworks of our own."

Len returned Cliff's wicked, naughty smile. "You're on. I should be finished in a few hours, though I'll need to get cleaned up before we go."

Len got back to work, the activity in and around the barn picking up as Nicole's students began to arrive for a class. The guys returned from the fields mid-afternoon, and Len sent them home for the day.

"We'll be in to check on the cattle in the morning." Then they were gone, driving away with huge smiles on their faces.

Nicole agreed to make sure the barn was in order when she left, so Len grabbed his bag from his car and went inside, finding Cliff in his office working on his paperwork.

"Let me get cleaned up quick, and we can go into town."

Cliff checked his watch. "Isn't it a little early?"

"For dinner, yes, but I want to stop at the drugstore and the dime store, if that's okay."

Cliff put down his papers. "We can stop wherever you like. I'm tired of this anyway. Go get cleaned up while I get Geoff up from his nap, and we can go." Len would have loved for Cliff to join him in the shower, but with no one to watch Geoff, it just wasn't practical.

Stripping off his clothes, he stepped into the shower and did a quick wash and scrub before stepping out, toweling off, and changing into clean clothes. When he was done, he did a quick cleanup of the bathroom and put his dirty clothes in his bag before stepping out into the hall. He could hear Geoff and Cliff talking in Geoff's room, probably as his clothes were being changed. "We're gonna go to the store with Len and then get some dinner."

"Bwench bwies?"

"Yes, you can get French fries." Len stood in the doorway and watched as Cliff finished getting Geoff dressed. When he was done, Cliff picked Geoff up and lifted him in the air, making airplane noises as he flew him around the room. Geoff instinctively put his arms out like wings as he and his father played a game they'd obviously played many times before. Cliff flew Geoff over to Len and placed him in has arms.

"Wen, hossey wide?"

"Not right now, Geoff. We're going into town. But if you're good, we'll get you a surprise." Cliff looked at Len, his eyes questioning. "I was thinking that Geoff needs a P-O-O-L for the summer." Geoff looked from Len to Cliff and back to Len, trying to puzzle out what they were talking about.

"Oh, he does, does he?" A tummy was tickled lightly. "Well, only if he's good." All three of them laughed as Geoff tried to squirm away from his dad's tickling fingers. "Let's go, shall we?" Len carried Geoff down the stairs, blowing a raspberry on his tummy, to the boy's delight, as they reached the bottom.

Through the house and out the back door, they walked and bounced to Geoff's delight until they reached the truck. Cliff buckled him in the seat as a car pulled into the drive. "Aun' Mawi,"

Geoff squealed, and he tried to get out of his seat, but he was already buckled in, so he had to wait impatiently until she leaned in the truck for a hug.

"Hi, Mari, what brings you by?"

"I was just driving past and saw you outside, so I thought I'd stop."

"We goin for bwench bwies." Geoff's little legs kept kicking the front of his seat.

"You are, huh? Then I better not keep you." Len got in the truck while Cliff walked his sister back to her car. He knew they were probably talking about Janelle, but he didn't want to interrupt. They appeared to finish quickly, and Mari waved to them as she got in her car and drove away.

"Daddy, wet's go. Bwench bwies." His little legs were swinging to beat the band.

"Okay, we're going." Cliff got in and buckled up before starting the truck and heading to town.

THE three of them did their shopping and then drove to the Dairy Barn for dinner. The purchases, including a kiddie pool and floaty toys, were tied down in the back of the truck.

The restaurant was busy, but there were a few empty tables, and they sat down and waited for their server. When no one showed up right away, Cliff glanced around the restaurant. "Why's everyone looking at us?"

Len shrugged and glanced at the people around them. It was true, they weren't trying to be too obvious, but they were obviously the objects of attention. "I think word may have gotten around town."

"Hi, I'm Steve," he looked around the table, his smile remaining genuine. "Does he need a booster seat?"

"That'd be great." He left and brought a plastic booster for Geoff. Cliff ordered for him and Geoff, but Len couldn't help glancing around the room.

Their server must have noticed. "They're just nosy." He said a little loudly, and everyone went back to their food. "Seems you're the latest bit of gossip." He rolled his eyes and lowered his voice. "You'd think they had nothing better to do than nose around in other people's lives."

Len placed his order and did his best to ignore the other diners, who for the most part had returned to their own conversations. Steve hustled away to get their order in and bring the drinks. "Well, at least we know what Janelle's been doing."

"I think so." Cliff appeared uncomfortable, and Len didn't exactly like being the center of attention himself. "I should have expected something like this."

"Let's not dwell on it and just enjoy our meal, okay?"

Cliff said he'd try and talked while they waited for their food.

"Here you go, guys." Steve brought the food and put the plates in front of them. "You aren't hiring by any chance, are you?" Cliff looked at Len in surprise. "I'm trying to get money together for college, and I could use another part-time job for the summer. I can't get enough hours here."

"Stop out after the holiday, and we'll talk," Len said. Steve refilled the water glasses and then left.

"Well, what do you know?" Len commented.

They started eating and were about halfway through their meal when the couple in the next booth got up to leave. They had to be in their seventies. Len saw the husband walk to the register, but the woman planted herself at the end of their table. "You boys should be ashamed of yourself."

Cliff looked up from his meal. "Excuse me?"

"I said—" self-righteousness flowing from her like a river, "—you should be ashamed of yourselves behaving that way."

Cliff was rendered speechless and sat gaping up at her. Len on the other hand, had had his fill of people like her. "I don't think so. You, on the other hand, should be ashamed of your behavior. So just climb on your broom and fly back to Oz." She had nothing to say to that. Whirling on her heels, she stuck her nose in the air and walked away as Len did his best Margaret Hamilton. "I'll get you my pretty and your little dog too!"

Cliff snickered, and even Geoff laughed as he ate and waved around a French fry. "Where did that come from?"

"Tim used to call it being campy. I heard him say that once, and it just popped out." Len tried to look all innocent, but his eyes sparkled too much to pull it off. "If they can dish it out, so can I."

Cliff and Len were still smiling as they finished their dinners and Steve brought the check. "Have a good night, guys."

Cliff took the check and got up to pay. "You too, Steve. We'll see you soon." The young waiter smiled and nodded before hurrying to his next table. Cliff paid the bill while Len left the tip, returning to get Geoff and gather their things. "Let's get him home." Len followed Cliff to the truck, getting in, and helping get Geoff buckled in his seat. "I had no idea people could be like that," Cliff commented.

Love Means ... *Courage*

The headiness of the confrontation had worn off, and a tinge of fear crept into him. Sure, he could take on an old lady, but what if it had been a stronger man or a group of men? What would he do then? "That was tame by comparison to some of the things Tim told me about. We need to be careful."

"This is Scottville. How dangerous could it be?"

Len remembered some of the things he'd heard when he was in high school, how cold people could be, how unaccepting. Yes, this was Scottville, but it wasn't a utopia where everyone accepted each other. This was real life, and there were people who'd be threatened by them.

"I don't know. Maybe I'm exaggerating, but we shouldn't take chances, especially with Geoff." Len was quiet as Cliff drove.

That seemed to wipe away some of Cliff's frivolousness. "Okay, we'll be careful. Does that mean we won't go to the fireworks?"

"We need to be careful, not hermits. We stick together and watch out for each other."

"I like watching your back." Cliff's eyes twinkled as he looked over at Len with a rather feral look on his face. Len quivered, but the innuendo didn't have its usual effect. He felt himself sinking into his own thoughts and worries.

"What are you thinking about?"

Len shook his head. "I don't want to make you angry. But I couldn't live with myself if anything happened to Geoff because of me, because I'm in your life."

Cliff pulled the truck into the drive and slammed it into park, jerking it to a stop. "I thought we already covered this." Cliff's eyes blazed with frustration and anger.

Len just sat there and looked down at his feet for a while, and then he lifted his eyes. "We did, and I haven't changed my mind. I'm just scared that someone might try to hurt either of you." Then it hit him, hard, and he swallowed the lump that threatened to rise in his throat. He didn't have the words for it, and he couldn't quite understand it, but the feelings were so strong.

Cliff got out of the truck, and Len followed deep in thought, stepping to the tailgate bed and pulling out their purchases. He set Geoff's new pool near his sandbox in a spot that would get plenty of sun before putting a little water in it to weigh it down. "Simmin." Geoff raced to the pool and was about to get in clothes and all before Cliff scooped him into his arms. "Simmin, Daddy."

"You can go swimming tomorrow. Right now, it's time for bed." Cliff unlocked the back door and carried a suddenly fussy Geoff inside while Len unloaded the rest of the purchases and followed them into the house.

Cliff got Geoff ready for bed while Len sat in the living room, alone with his thoughts. He heard Cliff come down the stairs. "You okay?"

"I will be."

Cliff sat next to him on the sofa. He felt arms slide around him and tug him against Cliff's chest. "We'll be okay. We're not the first to deal with this, and we won't be the last."

Len shifted to look at Cliff. "I know. But this could cost your relationship with your sister, make people hate you, and even cause problems for the farm."

"Shhh… I know that." Cliff put his hand on the back of Len's neck and drew him closer. "It doesn't matter. We'll handle it together." Then he felt Cliff's lips on his and the problems and worries slipped away. "I love you, Len."

Love Means ... *Courage*

He rested his head against Cliff's chest, a steady heartbeat in his ear. "Let's go upstairs." Len shifted before getting to his feet. Cliff got up as well and led Len to the bedroom. Len slipped off his clothes and slid beneath the covers, with Cliff following shortly behind him. "Just hold me, Cliff." Arms slid around him, pulling him close, Cliff's chest to Len's back, as lips skimmed over his neck. Cliff was right. All that mattered was the man holding him right now and the little boy sleeping in the next room. This was what mattered. In Cliff's arms, the worries slipped away, carried off by the sound of the crickets outside the open window serenading them as they drifted off to sleep.

SOMETHING wasn't right. Len sat up in bed, his head turning from side to side. Cliff was sound asleep, snoring lightly. Through the open window, he heard a horse whinny and then another. "Cliff, wake up!" He shook his lover hard. "Something's happening." Len was out of bed before the words were out of his mouth. Pulling on his jeans, he yanked on his shoes and took off out the bedroom door and down the stairs, toward the back door, flipping on lights in the house as he went.

Bursting out the back door, he heard horses and saw one running out the barn door and into the farmyard. Len flipped on the outside lights, bathing the yard and the front of the barn in a warm glow. "What the hell's going on?" Another horse ran from the barn, followed by two men.

Crack!

A loud shot rang out, and Len turned around. Cliff was standing on the steps, a shotgun pointed in the air. The men raced across the yard toward the road, hats flying off their heads. Car doors slammed, and an engine started and gunned. They could hear the wheels on the gravel as the car took off down the road.

"Go check on Geoff. I'll see about getting the horses." Len ran toward the barn. A few of the stall doors were open, but the horses were still inside. Shutting the stall doors, he closed the barn door as a precaution and grabbed a few carrots before walking across the yard. One of the horses was near the equipment shed. Len approached slowly, not wanting to spook the already agitated horse. "That's a good boy." Holding out his hand, he offered the carrot and got a hold on the halter, leading him back into the barn and into his stall.

"How bad is it?" Cliff walked into the barn, still carrying his gun and handing Len a shirt.

"I think it was just the two horses. I've already got one back in his stall, but the other one could be a ways away." Len closed the stall door. "How's Geoff?" Len slipped the shirt over his shoulders.

"Still asleep, thank God." Cliff relaxed slightly.

"Stay with him. I have to find Thunder." Len hurriedly saddled Misty. He led her into the yard and settled into the saddle. "He could hurt himself if I don't find him. I'll be back as soon as I find him."

"Hold on a minute." Cliff went in the barn, returning a minute later, holding Thunder's halter. "You'll need this." He handed Len the halter. "Where are you going to look?"

"He headed off across the street, so I'm going to try to follow. Hopefully he's still on the grounds of the community college." Len coaxed Misty into a trot, and they headed off into the night. Across the street from the farm was the wooded campus of West Shore Community College. Their parking lots were lit, so as long as Thunder stayed on the campus, there was a chance Len would be able to find him. Len pointed Misty along the edge of the drive, looking and listening intently.

Love Means ... Courage

Together, he and Misty roamed the parking lot and paths of the college until he saw a dark shape against one of the buildings. Len dismounted and led Misty forward, hoping the familiar horse would help calm the agitated stallion. As he got close, he could hear Thunder snorting and blowing out of his nose. "It's okay, boy. It's just me and Misty." Len pulled out a carrot and held it in his hand for Thunder to see. Len kept talking and slowly walked closer. To Len's relief, Thunder went for the carrot, and Len patted his neck as he slipped the halter over his head. Then he led both Misty and Thunder back toward the farm, walking through the quiet and deserted campus.

The first light was beginning to appear in the sky when Len and the two horses walked across the farmyard and into the barn. Len got Thunder into his stall and munching hay before walking Misty to hers and giving her another carrot. "You were a big help, girl." Removing the saddle and blanket, he put them away and closed the barn doors before walking back to the house.

He tried to be quiet as he closed the back door behind him, walking through the house and up the stairs. Cliff was awake in bed with the light on. "Did you find him?"

"Yes. He was at the far side of the college, but he's back in the barn now."

"Good. Come back to bed." Cliff lifted the covers.

"Cliff, it's almost time to get up."

"The chores will wait a few hours." Len stripped off his clothes and climbed back beneath the covers, Cliff's arms enfolding him, pulling him close. "Thank you for finding Thunder."

"You're welcome." The words barely passed Len's lips and he was asleep.

LEN woke to the bed shaking. "Wen! Wake up, Wen!" Geoff bounced on the bed and as soon as he cracked his eyes open, he saw Geoff's peering back at him. "Hossey wide."

The kid had a one-track mind. "Where's Daddy?"

"Right here." Cliff walked in the bedroom, fully dressed and a little dirty.

"Hosseys, Wen, hosseys."

"I take it you and Daddy were doing chores?"

"He insisted on helping, although most of his help consisted of feeding them carrots." Cliff handed him a mug of coffee, and Len sipped it slowly.

"Thank you. Is everything okay?"

"Yeah, they didn't do anything except let the horses out, and they left us a little present." Cliff reached around the door frame and produced a couple hats. "In their haste to leave, they left these behind."

"Did you call the police?" Before Cliff could answer, Geoff got up and began jumping on the bed. "That's enough, Geoffy." Len put his mug on the nightstand and threw back the covers, scooping Geoff into his arms to fits of laughter. "Let's get something to eat." Len put Geoff down and pulled on a clean pair of jeans and a light shirt before picking up his coffee and following them downstairs and into the kitchen.

The table was already set with a great cold summer breakfast. "We thought we'd surprise you after all the excitement last night." Cliff put Geoff in his chair and put his bowl on the tray.

"So what's the plan for today?" Len began filling his plate.

"There's some work to be done, and then we're going into town for lunch." Len looked skeptical but waited for Cliff to continue. "You know that Steve's is gossip central in this town, so we're going there for lunch. I'm thinking we're going to spread a little of our own gossip." The glint in Cliff's eye was making Len horny.

"Are you going to tell me what you've got on your mind?" Len asked as he ate a fat, juicy strawberry.

"Nope, you'll just have to come along and find out."

"What about Geoff?"

"Aunt Mari's coming by to watch him while he's in the P-O-O-L."

"What does she think about your idea?"

"Haven't told her. This is about you and me, and we need to handle it. Show them we're not afraid and stare them down—get them to blink first. They don't have to accept us, but they will understand that we won't take any crap." Len wasn't as sure as Cliff, but he was willing to trust him.

When breakfast was finished, Cliff shooed Len out of the kitchen, so he went out to the barn to get to work. They guys were already busy, so Len got to work, cleaning up the mess he'd left the night before, and then he got started on the never-ending task of cleaning stalls. The horses were already out, so Len figured Cliff had taken care of that while he was still in bed.

Len greeted Nicole and her students as they arrived for their lessons, got hay from the loft, and made sure all the tack was put away.

"Len, Mari's here. You about ready to go?" Cliff stood in the doorway, his body silhouetted against the sunshine outside the barn.

"Just a minute." He finished up and met Cliff by his truck. "You got this planned out?"

"Yup, just let me do the talking." They got in the truck, and Cliff drove into town, parking right in front of Steve's.

Len noticed the hats on the floor of the truck. "Are you taking these?" He reached for them when Cliff nodded. Getting out of the truck, they strode into Steve's and sat at the nearest table. Len saw Shell, and she walked toward their table.

"Your kind isn't welcome here!" Len turned his head and look into the eyes of a huge kid.

"And what kind is that?" Len heard Cliff's voice carrying through the room. "Paying customers? Or maybe this place is only for good-for-nothing loafers like you."

"Fags. We don't want fags here."

Cliff stood up, staring the kid in the eye, obviously conscious that every eye in the room was on him. "And who's we, Henry? You and the friend who paid us a visit last night?" Cliff picked up the hats from the seat next to him. "You two ran away in such a hurry you left your hats behind and a brown streak across my lawn. I'd sure hate to be the one to do your laundry." Soft laughter could be heard throughout the restaurant. Cliff held the two hats up high for everyone to see and then placed the one on the kid's head. "I suggest you leave before someone calls the police and has you arrested."

"This ain't over!"

"Yes, it is." Cliff turned to all the people in the room. "Everyone here has heard what you did and the threats you've implied. If anything happens, we'll know right where to look." Cliff handed Henry the other hat. "Give this to Jasper. He'll be looking for it."

Love Means ... *Courage*

Henry looked around the room and found a whole lot of people doing their best not to meet his eyes. Seeing his support gone, he turned and left the restaurant.

Cliff sat back down in his chair and motioned to Shell. "I don't think we'll have any more trouble."

Shell came over and took their orders with a brighter smile than usual before moving on. Gradually the room returned to its normal conversation level. Both of them had no doubt that they were the topic of most of the conversations. "Are you sure?" Len looked around the room and saw others meeting his gaze instead of looking away.

"Yes. They may not understand, but they respect us for having the courage to stand up for ourselves."

Shell brought their lunches, setting their plates in front of them. "That was sweet, the way you handled Henry, and Steve said to tell you that you are welcome here any time."

They exchanged smiles and began to eat. Throughout lunch, Len noticed that people would nod or smile as they passed the table. "Let's finish our lunch and get back to the farm."

"That's fine with me. I feel like I'm on display," Cliff agreed.

Len did his best to ignore that attention and ate his lunch. When they were finished, they paid their bill, being sure to leave a generous tip, and left the restaurant.

"Is there anything you need while we're here?"

"No, let's get back to the farm, I've got work to do, and you need to check on the fields to make sure everything's okay." Cliff nodded, and they got in the truck.

"I think it's going to be fine, Len. That doesn't mean we won't have trouble in the future, but hopefully we won't have a repeat of last night anytime soon." Cliff started the truck and pointed it back toward the farm, a hand on Len's leg.

CHAPTER 18

"ARE you ready to see the fireworks?" Cliff tossed Geoff in the air and then hugged him close, father and son playing their own happy games. Cliff looked at Len. "Is the car seat ready?"

"Yup, and I've got a bag of drinks and snacks in the trunk along with blankets and a few of Geoff's cars."

"Then let's go." Cliff was just about to shut the door when the phone rang. Handing Geoff to Len, he went back inside, and Len carried Geoff to the car, buckling him into his seat.

"Daddy should be here in a few minutes, and then we can go." Geoff was excitedly bouncing his heels against his seat. The passenger door opened, and Cliff climbed into the car and they started toward town.

"That was Mari; she's going to meet us there."

"So are Mom and Jerry. This should be fun." Len drove carefully because of all the traffic heading toward the fireworks. As they got closer, traffic got heavier, and they lined up to get into the parking area. Len rolled down his window and made a donation to the fireworks fund before pulling into the spot designated by one of the men in orange vests. Getting out, Cliff got Geoff, and Len grabbed the supplies from the trunk. Then they walked to what was usually the football practice field.

Families had spread their blankets all over the lawn, and Len looked for his mother and Jerry in the fading light, finding them near the middle of the throng. They'd saved them a place, and Len spread the blanket and they sat down. After making introductions, Len got out Geoff's toys, and the toddler began running them around the blanket. They talked until Mari approached and settled on the blankets. Cliff introduced her to Lorna and Jerry, and Geoff pulled on Len's sleeve, pointing to the ice cream truck. Cliff stood up. "I'm going for ice cream, what would everyone like?" Orders were given, and Cliff began to thread through the maze of blankets.

"I'll go with you." Getting up, Mari began making her way as well. Geoff settled in Len's lap, running his cars up and along his arm.

"I always hoped you'd have children." Lorna said regretfully.

"I know, Mom. You always wanted to be a grandmother." He turned his head toward the ice cream truck and saw Cliff and Mari waiting in line, deep in conversation.

"Len!" He turned, realizing Lorna was speaking to him.

"Sorry."

"I was asking how things were going?"

Len sighed. "We had a little trouble at the Dairy Barn the other night." He told her about the woman confronting them. He also told her what he'd said, and both Lorna and Jerry doubled over with laughter.

"Serves her right for being a busybody," Jerry said as his laughter subsided. "Sometimes I wonder what people are thinking."

Love Means ... *Courage*

"So do I." Geoff began squirming, and Len saw Cliff and Mari coming back, carrying the ice cream goodies. Len noticed that Cliff looked about ready to explode. His face was red, and his arms were shaking. He handed out the ice cream before sitting on the blanket, taking Geoff and settling him on his lap. To say there was something wrong was an understatement, and Len watched as Cliff opened Geoff's ice cream sandwich and gave him half, eating the other half himself. "What is it, Cliff?"

To Len's surprise, he shook his head and looked like he was blinking back tears. He managed to croak a quick, "I'll tell you later," and returned his attention to Geoff, who was happily devouring his ice cream.

Boom!

Geoff jumped and looked up as the first shell burst in the sky, and then one after another left its trail of colored sparks and light. Geoff pointed at each one, looking around as if to make sure everyone else saw the wondrous things he was seeing. Len barely noticed the fireworks—his attention was on Cliff and the way his jaw was set and how his anger had faded only to be replaced by what looked like fear. He looked to Mari, but she was intently watching the fireworks.

When the boom of the last shell reverberated over the crowd, people clapped, and then the crowd all seemed to lift to their feet as one. Belongings were gathered, and everyone began wandering back to their cars. Len hugged and said goodbye to his mother and shook Jerry's hand before the older couple walked to their car. Mari stayed with Cliff and Len as they walked toward the cars. Geoff rested against his father, head on his shoulder, almost immediately falling asleep.

Both Len and Cliff said goodbye to Mari when they got to the parking lot, and she hugged both of them before walking to her car. Len desperately wanted to ask what was going on, but he remained patient until they got Geoff into his seat and the stuff stowed in the trunk. "What happened?"

"I'll tell you at home, once he's in bed. I don't want him to hear the swearing, and there'll be plenty of it."

Holy shit, what was going on? Len climbed in the car and drove back to the farm. Cliff stared blankly out the window—no conversation, no furtive looks, nothing. This was so unusual that Len was beginning to wonder if *he'd* done something to make Cliff so angry.

Parking his car in his usual spot, he started unloading as Cliff took Geoff inside and straight upstairs to his bed. Len brought the things into the house and put them away as best he could. He was finishing up when he heard Cliff come down the stairs. With a little trepidation, he met him in the living room.

Cliff looked pale as he sat on the sofa. Len sat next to him, and he was immediately pulled into a hug and felt Cliff's chest heaving against him. "She's going to try to take Geoff away from me."

Len wasn't sure he'd heard right. "Who is?"

"Janelle. That's what Mari was telling me when we were getting ice cream." Cliff lifted himself away from Len, looking like he was ready to be sick. "Mari wasn't able to get in touch with Janelle, but she talked to Vikki. And she said that Janelle had gotten a lawyer and was going to try to sue me for custody because I was bringing Geoff up in an immoral household."

"How can she do that?" Len could barely believe his ears. "That mean-spirited, spiteful bitch!"

Cliff smiled for a split second. "I told you there'd be swearing."

"You're damn right. There's no way she's going to take Geoff away from you." Len stood and began pacing the room before stopping in front of Cliff. "Did Mari say how Vikki felt?"

Cliff put his arms around Len's waist, resting his head against his stomach. "According to her, she was appalled. I think Vikki reacted the same way she would if Janelle were trying to take the baby she's about to have away from her."

"If you want my advice, I think all three of you need to confront her. She needs to realize that none of you support her, and that if she tries this, the rest of her family will stand against her. That might be enough to get her to back down."

Cliff sighed. "We can only try." The phone rang, and Cliff let go of Len and answered it. "Yeah, she told me." Cliff's face remained the same. "We were just talking about that." Len sat on the sofa and waited. "Okay, I'll see you then." Cliff smiled briefly. "Let's hope so… and thank you." Cliff hung up the phone and sank onto the sofa. "That was Vikki. She, Janelle, and Mari are going to be here tomorrow. She said she'd drag Janelle out here if she had to."

"Do you think she'll actually come?"

"Vikki and Janelle have always been allies, even as children. Vikki must feel very strongly about this, so yeah, she'll come if Vikki wants her to."

Cliff looked drained, and Len pulled him close, just holding him. "Come on, let's go to bed." This time, Len led Cliff toward the bedroom, and it was Len's turn to cradle Cliff in *his* arms. Getting ready for bed, Len pulled a distressed and very scared lover close. "No one's going to take Geoffy, not if I can help it." Len held Cliff and rocked him gently as he clung to him like a lifeline, until exhaustion and worry took their toll and sleep took hold.

"CLIFF?" Len sat up in the empty bed, the house nearly pitch black, quiet, and very still. Pushing back the blankets, he pulled on his boxers and left the room. Padding down the hall in his bare feet, he saw that Geoff's door was open and peeked inside. Cliff's familiar shape was sitting in the chair next to his son's bed, watching him sleep. "Cliff." His head lifted and turned to look toward the whisper. "Come back to bed."

He got a nod in response and slowly got up. Len took his hand, leading him back to the bedroom. He could feel the fear in the way Cliff held his hand and in the way he shuffled his feet. "It's gonna be okay." Len helped Cliff back into bed, tenderly removing his lover's boxers. He'd done this so many times before, but this time, the action was tender and caring as opposed to sexy. Slipping off his own, he slid between the covers, pulling Cliff to him, their skin touching in tenderness and caring, Len soothing Cliff's fear.

"I don't know what I'd do if anything happened to him... to either of you." Cliff's voice was rough, like he'd been crying. Len stroked Cliff's hair and face, his fingers drawing irregular shapes across his cheek as he felt his heart expand within his chest. That one simple statement erased all Len's own fears. In his mind, Cliff had extended his family to include him, creating something he never thought he'd have: a family of his own.

Len whispered into his lover's ear. "I won't let anyone hurt our family." Cliff rolled over and pulled Len to him, a hand cradling his head. Their legs entwined, chests meeting, as lips found their companions in the dark.

WHEN morning light gleamed through the open window, Len again found himself alone in the bed. This time, he instinctively knew where Cliff was. Opening the closet door, he put on one of Cliff's robes and went down the hall to Geoff's room. Cliff was asleep in the chair next to Geoff's bed. Smiling to himself, he turned around and dressed before leaving the house as quietly as he could. Len went to the barn and got to work. Because of the holiday, there were extra things to get done.

"Len, are you in here?" He stuck his head out of the stall he was working on and saw Cliff carrying Geoff, still in his pajamas, head resting on his daddy's shoulder, eyes only half open.

"Morning. Just finishing here." Cliff walked to him and adjusted Geoff so he could lean forward slightly and give Len a kiss.

"Mari called. My sisters should be here in a few hours."

"Okay. I'll make myself scarce while they're here." Len wasn't about to interfere in what he saw as a private family matter.

"I want you there, Len." Cliff shuffled his feet. "That is, if you'll…." He floundered for words.

"I'll be there, if that's what you want."

Cliff put a hand on the back of Len's neck, drawing him into a hard kiss. "I want you with me forever." Len returned the kiss, the words still ringing in his ears. Had Cliff meant what he thought he meant? His questions died away as Cliff deepened the kiss, possessively ravishing his mouth before lightening the kiss and stepping away, keeping his hand on Len's neck, fingers lightly stroking his skin. "Come inside in a while, and I'll have breakfast ready."

"Okay." He couldn't think of anything else to say, so he watched Cliff's back as he left the barn, Geoff sleepily smiling at him over his father's shoulder.

Putting away the tools, Len went to the loft and dropped the hay he'd need through one of the trap doors. Back downstairs he stacked the hay near the stalls before slipping off his gloves and walking toward the house.

Geoff was already in his seat, and Cliff was just about ready to dish up the hearty pancake breakfast. "How are you going to handle things when your sisters get here?" Len asked.

Cliff brought the food to the table and poured glasses of orange juice. "I think I'm going to let Mari and Vikki do most of the talking. They'll probably be more effective than I will. Besides, it'll be easier for me to keep my temper in check, because I know I'll start yelling at her. What about you?"

Len took a few pancakes from the stack before adding butter and syrup. "I'm going to sit in the back and keep quiet. I'm there to support you, but this is largely a matter between you and your sister." Geoff reached out toward Len's plate.

"Hang on, Geoff. Yours is coming." Cliff put a small plate on his tray, and Geoff picked up his baby fork and began shoveling in bits of syrup-covered pancake, grinning as he chewed.

Cliff passed the sausage with a slight tremble in his hand. Len noticed but didn't comment, knowing it was Cliff's nervousness, and maybe a touch of anger, escaping. Len ate heartily, but Cliff picked at his food and fussed around Geoff, making sure he didn't make too big of a mess.

When they were done, they worked together to clean up, both the kitchen and Geoff before going outside. Cliff ran a hose to the basement and attached it to the wash sink, and Len used it to refill Geoff's pool, while the little prince himself watched with delight and only Len's vigilance kept him from jumping in, clothes and all. "Simmin, Wen, simmin."

"Once it warms up just a little bit more." Len signaled to Cliff, and he turned off the water and unhooked the hose. Len scooped Geoff off his feet, swinging him in his arms. "Wouldn't want you to be cold." Len blew a raspberry on Geoff's tummy, and he retaliated by blowing one on Len's cheek.

Their playing was interrupted by two cars pulling into the driveway. Mari got out of her car first, and Vikki wedged herself out of the other one, followed by Janelle, who'd driven—probably so she could make a getaway, if she had to. Cliff came out and met them at the door, ushering everyone inside. Mari helped Vikki while Janelle lingered behind, staring daggers at Len.

"Come on, Janelle." Vikki did nothing to conceal the annoyance in her voice as she waddled inside.

Janelle said nothing but made her feelings very clear with a sour look and walked inside. Len followed, carrying Geoff.

By the time he joined the group, they were settled in the living room. Len handed Geoff to Cliff and took a chair near the back of the room where Cliff could see him.

"We all know why we're here, so I'll just come to the point." Vikki reclined on the sofa and looked at Janelle. "The purpose of this family meeting is not to discuss this ridiculous notion of anyone trying to take away Cliff's son." She glared at Janelle, who unfortunately seemed impervious.

"I already have a lawyer who says I have a case based on moral grounds."

"You do not!" Vikki raised her voice only slightly. "What you have is a shyster who'll take your money. There's no way any court is going to take a perfectly happy child away from his father and give him to an unmarried spinster aunt. Particularly one with her own family testifying vehemently against her." Len was surprised at her intensity, but he figured Vikki had put herself in Cliff's place and it scared her. "And just so we're clear, if you do this, you are no longer family. Testifying in court will be the last time we ever see or speak to you." Vikki looked at Mari, who nodded her agreement.

Janelle's eyes grew big as saucers. That was obviously something that had never occurred to her. "But it's immoral."

"For God's sake, Janelle, it's 1984, not 1884. Who Cliff loves is none of your business, and while we're on the subject, who died and made you the morality police?"

Janelle's hackles were up, and she bristled under their rebuke but held herself straight and tall in the chair. She obviously hadn't given up, but Vikki didn't give her a chance. "We're here to discuss why you're acting this way." Vikki's voice became soothing and soft, speaking to Janelle. "You're obviously hurt and trying to get back at Cliff for something. And don't bother denying it. I grew up with you, remember?" Vikki looked at Janelle, who flinched for the first time. "What is it, Janie?"

Len looked at Cliff from where he sat and waited to see if Janelle would answer. He wasn't so sure she wouldn't just get up and leave. "How would you feel if you found out your boyfriend was in love with your brother?" She pulled a handkerchief out of her purse and dabbed her eyes, trying to keep herself from breaking down.

"He was never your boyfriend. And if you look at it objectively, you know Len was just a friend." Cliff kept his voice calm and did his best to mimic Vikki's tone. "Janie, you should be happy for him and for me. After Ruby died I was so lost, and Len helped me find my way again."

"By turning you gay!"

Cliff chuckled softly. "He didn't turn me gay. I've been gay for a long time. He just helped me gather the courage to admit it to myself and to my family. He loves me, Janie, and I love him."

Geoff squirmed, and Cliff let him down. Janelle sniffled, and Geoff walked to her and patted her leg. "Is okay, Aun' Nell, is okay."

Love Means ... *Courage*

"Janie, let it go." Vikki squirmed on the sofa, making a face. "You'll be much happier if you just let it go and move on."

"What is it?" Mari stood and took Vikki's hand, and she knew. "Cliff, would you call Dan? Tell him to meet Vikki at the hospital; she's going into labor." Mari helped her sister to her feet. "Janie, get your car started and pull it around to the front."

She nodded and got to her feet, but before she took a step, she was engulfed in a hug. "You'll be okay, Janie." Vikki let her go and began waddling toward the front door. Janelle headed out to the car, pulling it around to the door, and Vikki got into the passenger seat.

Cliff approached the car, and Vikki rolled down the window. "Dan's on his way." He leaned forward and kissed her on the cheek. "Thank you," he whispered into her ear, "You're going to be a terrific mother."

Vikki slid her hand down Cliff's cheek. "And you and Len are going to be terrific fathers." She slid her hand away, and the car pulled down the drive and onto the street.

CHAPTER 19

"CLIFF." He turned at the sound of Mari's voice. "You okay?" He nodded, not really seeing her, or anything, really. "Is anybody home?" She waved her hand in front of his face, "Earth to Cliff."

"Sorry. I was just thinking." Geoff ran across the yard, grabbing Cliff's leg, pointing at the pool.

"Simmin, Daddy." His face was tilted up, those eyes looking almost mournful.

Len joined the group. "I've got some work to finish up." He was about to walk away, but Cliff caught his eye, and he stopped.

Mari picked Geoff up. "Come on, I'll take you upstairs and get you ready for a swim. Daddy and Len have things to do."

"Simmin, yay!" he called as she carried him inside.

"What do you have to do?" Len started to rattle off the things on his list, but Cliff stopped him. "Steve's starting tomorrow, and he's going to need some things to do. Besides, I think we need to go for a ride."

Love Means ... *Courage*

"I'll saddle the horses."

"We won't need the horses." Len's eyes widened as he realized the kind of ride Cliff had in mind. "Come on." Cliff led him through the barn and around the riding ring to a trail that cut around one of the pastures. Cliff took Len's hand and guided them into the trees. The trail led to the creek and then turned, the water babbling as they walked. "I know I don't say what I'm feeling very often." They found themselves in a small clearing and Cliff stopped walking, dropping the blanket he'd grabbed on their way through the barn. "But I need to tell you now. You have to be the most patient man I've ever known. You waited five years for a second kiss, and you waited weeks for me to come to my senses and realize how important you are." Cliff spread the blanket on the grass, tugging Len down next to him as he knelt. "Just so you know, with no prodding and no drama, I love you, Len Parker, with everything I am." Len leaned forward, but Cliff stopped him with a touch and a smile. "I want to ask you to live with me, with us. The bed, the house, my life, they're all too lonely without you."

Len swallowed and nodded, unable to speak at that moment.

"Was that a yes?"

"Yes." Len looked down at the blanket. "I can hardly believe it." He looked up and saw Cliff's eyes gleaming in the sunlight. "I had a huge crush on you, ya know. Even before you kissed me." Len scooted closer, their knees touching as Cliff pulled their chests together. "I volunteered for the play because you were in it and that way I had an excuse to watch you."

"Sometimes I wonder what would have happened if Sheila hadn't interrupted our first kiss."

Len smiled and ghosted his lips over Cliff's neck. "I'm grateful to her." Cliff pulled back, looking into Len's eyes. "If she hadn't, who knows what might have happened. Instead, you married Ruby, loved her, and had Geoff. Everything happens for a reason.

And if you had it to do over again, knowing how things came out, would you change anything?"

"No." Cliff shook his head gently. "I have everything I could ever want. Well, almost everything."

Len waited suspiciously for a second, and then his lips were taken in an earth-stopping kiss as Cliff guided him back on the blanket. "I love you, Len Parker. I'm not very eloquent when it comes to things like this, and I don't have flowery words to tell you how I feel." Cliff's fingers worked the buttons on Len's shirt, pulling it open and baring the smooth chest to his hot gaze, and instead of words, he let his lips talk in other ways.

Len hissed softly as Cliff's lips sucked gently on one of his nipples, pulling more and more insistently as the suction grew more intense. "Cliff. God, Cliff." Len arched his back into the sensation.

Eyes shining, Cliff's eyes shifted to look up at Len. "You really like that, don't you?"

Len nodded as his other nipple was subjected to the same delicious torturous treatment. "Love you, Cliff." No one made his body sing the way his lover could. A few touches of his hands or hot lips on his skin, and he was soaring with delight.

"Love you, too, but talk is cheap. Let me show you how I love you." Len nodded again as Cliff opened Len's belt and slipped his pants off his legs, with his boxers following soon after.

"I know how you feel, Cliff." He felt his skin heat beneath his lover's almost feral gaze, and he throbbed against his stomach, knowing that he could put that look on his lover's face and that no one else would ever see that look except him. That piece of Cliff was all his.

"But you deserve to feel it." Len jumped slightly as he felt Cliff's hands on his leg, skidding lightly on the hair, lips following the hands, kissing the skin as it heated beneath Cliff's palms. He felt his legs stroked along his hip and up to his stomach. Len was so close; he thrust forward, trying to get Cliff to give him some attention. He thought of taking care of things himself but curled his hands into the blanket instead, knowing Cliff's attentions would be well worth it.

The weight on him disappeared, and he opened his eyes, watching as Cliff pulled his shirt over his head and slid his pants down his legs before stepping nude into the sun. Len looked his fill as his lover dropped something on the blanket. Then his lips were back, pummeling his mouth, hot skin pressing onto the earth beneath the blanket, warm skin sliding against him. "Cliff," he moaned, brushing his lover's hair from his eyes. "Please." He didn't know what he was asking for, just that he *needed*. Bringing Cliff's lips to his, he returned his lover's affection, losing himself in deep, passionate kisses that stole his breath away.

Cliff's eyes bored into him, and Len tremble beneath their gaze, so filled with love as they glistened with reflected sunlight. Cliff's lips trailed down his body, but their eyes remained glued to each others'.

Lips ghosted over his length, and he cried out softly as a zing traveled along his spine. Then Cliff's tongue swirled around his flared head, and he pushed forward, wanting Cliff's mouth so badly. Finally, it happened; Len was engulfed in hot wetness, taking him deep in one swift movement. "Cliff," he gasped, "love your mouth on me." A hand stroked Len's stomach, fingers tweaking a nipple, as he was again taken deep and hard. "Love you, Cliff." His stomach clenched, and he thrust hard, feeling as though Cliff was going to make his head explode as he kept him on a knife's edge. To make matters more frustrating, he could tell Cliff was enjoying this torture by the chorus of small moans and groans he was making.

Len pounded his fists into the ground, clenching and unclenching his hands until finally Cliff gave him what he needed.

"Cliff!" With a cry that filled the clearing and burst across the creek, he came, his release splitting his mind like a bolt of lightning.

As he came back to himself, he felt Cliff swallowing everything he'd pulled from him. Lying on the blanket like a wet rag, he expected Cliff to kiss him, but instead, his legs were lifted and his entrance exposed. Without mercy, Cliff began again, lips and tongue sliding along his crease. "Are you trying to kill me?"

"Can you think of a better way to go than to be loved to death?" Len couldn't think of *anything* as Cliff probed him with his tongue. He just sank into an oblivion of passion, his head rocking on the blanket, the sensations from Cliff's loving rolling over him in waves. His body was not his own; he belonged to Cliff just as Cliff belonged to him. Right here, right now, Cliff was claiming him, telling every fiber of his being, every synapse in his pleasurably short-circuited brain that he was his.

A long, thick finger sank into him, retreated, and sank deep again. Small whimpers turned to cries as the finger found what it was looking for and lights flashed behind Len's eyes.

"I can't wait any more."

"Don't wait, Cliff, take me. Take me now!" The finger slipped away, replaced by what Len really wanted. Slowly, relentlessly, he was stretched and filled. Their bodies joined as Cliff leaned forward, kissing him hard. Their eyes locked, and Cliff began to move.

"You belong to me. You're a part of me, now and always." Cliff kept moving deep inside him, sliding across the spot that made his head throb.

"Cliff." He could feel it building again, the desire that had barely flagged returning full force as he grasped his own length.

"Say it, Len. Say it with me. Forever."

Love Means ... *Courage*

"Yes… forever, Cliff! Forever and ever." He felt Cliff fill him, hot and deep, and his own body painted white streaks over his hand.

Breathing hard, Len felt every muscle in body go limp. Cliff pulled back, and he sighed as his lover slipped from his body. Then Cliff was there—kissing him, holding him, and saying sweet things that warmed his heart. Things meant only for him. Len returned the kisses gladly, ardently, as his eyes closed and his hands held on to Cliff like a security blanket.

The sun warmed their bodies as they dozed, the breeze rustling the trees. "Cliff." His lover's response was a sleepy grunt. "I think we should get up." The ground wasn't the most comfortable place for a nap, after all.

"I'm afraid you're right, but you feel so good, I never want to move." Cliff did, reluctantly, and they dressed, their touches and kisses slowing their progress immensely. Eventually, they made their way back down the path to the house. As they approached, they heard laughter and splashes. "Geoff must still be in the pool."

Len laughed. "You actually think he'd get out willingly?"

"Daddy! Wen!" Geoff saw them and climbed out of the pool, running barefoot across the grass. "I simmin."

Cliff swung him into the air. "Yes, you are, but it's time for lunch."

His little hands went to his hips. "Daddy! I simmin." As if swimming were the most important thing in the world.

"After lunch, you can swim some more, and Len will take you riding too." That placated him, and Cliff let him down, wrapping him in a towel before leading them inside. "Can you stay for lunch?" He looked at his sister.

"No, I have to go to the hospital. Dan called, and Vikki's still in labor."

"Should I go to the hospital with you?"

"No. Janelle and I will both be there. We'll call when we know more." She hugged Geoff, who was still wrapped in the towel. "I'll call you when we know more. Bye."

"Bye, Aun' Mawi."

Then she hugged both Cliff and Len. Cliff went inside, and Len walked her to her car. "Take good care of him." She looked toward the house. "Let us know if you need help moving." Len must have looked shocked, but Mari just winked and smiled. "Intuition." She said nothing more and got in her car, waving as she drove away.

THAT evening, Len climbed into bed next to his naked lover. "Did you see your mother?" Len smiled and nodded. "What'd she say?"

"She hugged me and told me to be happy. I was worried she'd be lonely, but she'd hear none of it and then helped me pack some of my things."

"Your mother is something else."

"That she is." Len kissed his lover, his life partner, and turned out the light as a faint, deep rumble could be heard in the distance. "It wasn't supposed to rain tonight."

"Tell that to the unpredictable Mother Nature."

Len slipped out from under the covers and drew on a pair of jeans, slipping into a pair of shoes. Cliff got out of bed as well. But Len said, "I've got this." Hurrying to the barn and opening the pasture doors, he whistled, and soon large heads appeared. Len led the horses to their stalls. Once they were all inside, he made sure they had fresh water and hay before closing the doors and walking back to the house. Lightning lit the horizon as he crossed the yard, and the thunder sounded again, this time closer and more insistent.

Len closed the door quietly behind him and crept up the stairs and into Cliff's... *their* bedroom. He was still not used to it being "theirs." Cliff turned on the light, sitting up, waiting for him. "Everything okay? I checked on Geoff, and he's sound asleep."

"Everything's fine. They were all ready to come in and went right to their stalls." Len slipped off his jeans, climbing back in bed, Cliff's arms drawing him close. They'd both agreed to wear boxers to bed for kid reasons.

"Mari just called. Vikki had a girl. They named her Jill."

"That's great! So, Geoff has a cousin." Cliff nodded against his skin, the beard rough and sexy. "Speaking of Geoff, do you think we'll have company?"

Cliff laughed as he kissed him. "We might." He clicked off the light.

Outside, the wind picked up, and they heard rain on the roof. Lightning flashed, and thunder clapped, and then the storm settled into a nice, steady rain. "Love you."

"Love you too." Len felt Cliff draw him to him, their lips finding each others' in the dark.

Epilogue

"Whose crazy idea was this anyway?" Len hung a piñata shaped like a horse in one of the trees in the yard.

Cliff called, "I believe it was yours," as he set the picnic table with the cowboy plates and cups, checking his watch.

"We still have time. Mari said she'd keep him busy until two. His friends will start arriving at one-thirty, so don't worry."

"I don't know why you insisted on a surprise birthday party."

Len stepped down and folded the ladder. "Because, unlike most kids, he's never asked for one, and I thought this one should be special. And besides, he can see all his friends from kindergarten."

"How'd you get a hold of everyone anyway?" Cliff finished up with the table and looked at his handiwork.

"Mari did, actually." There were some parents who hadn't wanted their kids to go to the party, but most of them had been great and accepted both Cliff and Len as Geoff's fathers.

Len put the ladder in the equipment shed. When he returned, he saw Fred, Randy, and Steve walking out of the barn with huge smiles on their faces. "You guys all set?"

"Yeah. I just need to go inside and change." Steve had agreed to dress up as a "real" cowboy and let the kids each have a turn riding Misty. "I thought I'd lead them around the drive and use the bench by the barn to help them on and off."

"I'm manning the grill." Fred unrolled an apron that said: "Don't kiss the cook, he's taken."

Randy laughed when he saw it. "And I'm on game duty." They had plastic horseshoes and a cowboy-themed bean-bag toss.

"Good." Len headed inside and returned with the drink cooler. "Let's get the last of it ready."

They finished the preparations as the first of the kids and their parents began to arrive. Dan and Vikki arrived with Geoff's cousins, Jilly and baby Chris, a few minutes later. Soon the yard was filled with five-year-old boys and girls running and playing. The phone rang, and Cliff answered it. After hanging up, he announced, "Geoff will be here in a few minutes, so everybody hide."

The guys helped the kids, and Cliff waited until Mari pulled into the drive. Geoff got out and looked around. Cliff gave the signal, and everyone jumped out and yelled, "Surprise!"

Geoff screamed with delight and then raced across the yard to join his friends. Steve brought out Misty, and the party started, with kids playing games and riding the horse until the food was ready, which was followed by cake and ice cream.

Then it was time for presents. Geoff sat at the table and opened each gift, thanking the giver, just like Len had taught him. Cliff looked so proud. Len thought he was going to burst. Once he'd opened everything, the party died down, and parents began to arrive to take everyone home.

Once the kids were gone, Len motioned to Steve, who quietly disappeared into the barn.

Cliff looked at his son. "Geoff, Len and I wanted to get you something special for your birthday." Steve emerged from the barn.

"You got me a pony!" Geoff was jumping up and down with excitement as Steve walked the small horse to where Geoff stood.

"Yes. His name is Raspberry, and Len is going to give you riding lessons." Geoff gave his dad a big hug and then raced to Len, throwing himself into his arms for a hug as well. Len carried Geoff to the pony and placed him in the saddle. Taking the reins from Steve, Len led Geoff and Raspberry around the yard as Geoff whooped and laughed.

"Let me get a picture of the three of you." Steve went to his truck and got his camera. Len held Raspberry's reins, and Cliff stood near Geoff, all three of them waiting as Steve focused the camera. "Say cheese." They smiled, and the shutter clicked—a family portrait.

Now available from Dreamspinner Press

The sequel to *Love Means... Courage*

Geoff is in the city, living the gay life to the hilt, when his father's death convinces him to return to the family farm. Discovering a young Amish man asleep in his barn, Geoff learns that Eli is spending a year away from the community before accepting baptism into the church. Despite their mutual attraction, Geoff is determined not to become involved with him, but Eli has discovered that Geoff shares his feelings and begins to court him, neatly capturing first Geoff's attention and then his heart.

Their budding relationship is threatened by closed-minded, gossipy relatives and the society at large, a whole new world to Eli, and he must decide whether to return to the community, his family, and the world and future he knows or to stay with Geoff and have faith in the power of love.

Also Available from Dreamspinner Press

Don't miss these other exciting titles

by ANDREW GREY

ANDREW GREY grew up in western Michigan with a father who loved to tell stories and a mother who loved to read them. Since then he has lived throughout the country and traveled throughout the world. He has a master's degree from the University of Wisconsin-Milwaukee and works in information systems for a large corporation. Andrew's hobbies include collecting antiques, gardening, and leaving his dirty dishes anywhere but in the sink (particularly when writing). He considers himself blessed with an accepting family, fantastic friends, and the world's most supportive and loving partner. Andrew currently lives in beautiful historic Carlisle, Pennsylvania.

Visit his Web Site at http://www.andrewgreybooks.com and his blog at http://andrewgreybooks.livejournal.com/.

Lightning Source UK Ltd.
Milton Keynes UK
02 December 2010

163794UK00009B/158/P